FALL OF THE ULTRAS

MATT BLAKE

MATTBLAKEAUTHOR.COM

The characters and events portrayed in this book are fictitious. Any similarity to real persons, living or dead, is coincidental and not intended by the author. Any reference to real locations is only for atmospheric effect, and in no way truly represents those locations.

Cover design by Damonza

If you want to be notified when Matt Blake's next novel is released, please sign up to his mailing list.

http://mattblakeauthor.com/newsletter

Your email address will never be shared and you can unsubscribe at any time.

[1]

I felt the grip tightening around my neck and I knew I didn't have long left.

All around me, there was darkness. Total darkness, so black it was suffocating. Just looking at that darkness made me feel a wave of sickness and light-headedness, in the way a young kid feared the dark at night. The same reason they begged their parents to keep a night light on for them. There were always monsters in the dark, in the mind of a kid.

Except right now, there really was a monster in this darkness.

The grip tightened even harder around my neck. I kicked back, reflexively more than anything. There was nothing else I could do, not really. I'd tried sparking my powers. I'd tried firing my way free of this mess. All of it was to no avail.

I was trapped. And the life was slipping away from me by the second.

I heard the blasts all around me, accompanied by the screams, and the feeling of sickness deep within grew even more intense. A bitter taste of blood and vomit filled my mouth, making me want to cough. I could smell something in the air. I couldn't describe it any other way than a thickness. Like the air was filled with tar, and that thickness was getting even more slimy, making breathing gradually more difficult.

But it was the eyes that scared me more than anything.

There was nothing grandiose about these eyes. There was nothing menacing about them, to the average person. It was their familiarity that got to me more than anything. I'd looked into these eyes before, a number of times. I'd stared into them, and they'd stared back at me.

And now they were the eyes that were looking at me as I struggled for my final breaths.

"It's over," the deep, gruff voice said. "Don't fight it. This is the only way it happens. This is the way it's always happened. Just... release."

I didn't want to stop fighting, as much as giving up any resistance would be the easy option here. So I gritted my teeth and kept my focus on those eyes, like I had so many times already. "N... never."

The hand around my neck loosened just enough for me to catch some breath. I coughed, then I felt vomit trickling up and out of my mouth, stilling my quest for a good lungful of air.

When I'd spewed up, the grip tightened once again, and I was pinned back hard against a solid wall.

As I was held there, I wondered what I had done to deserve this life. I was Kyle Peters. I wasn't even in my twenties, and yet somehow, I was the strongest ULTRA in existence—at least people thought, and at least people expected. I didn't *ask* to be Glacies. Glacies just became me.

I'd been dealt these cards, and now I was being forced to live with them. Now, I was being forced to accept who I was. But also something else.

I was being forced to accept that I wasn't as strong as I'd hoped—or as the world hoped—all along.

"All these years of resisting instead of living," the voice said. "Now, it's time to stop. It's time to hand yourself over. So stop resisting, Kyle. End the pain. For yourself. For your family."

The mention of my family made me feel a warmth deep inside. But it was a warmth tinged with sadness. After all, my family had been torn apart, all because of me. It had been decimated, all because of me.

I felt a tear roll down my cheek when I thought of Ellicia, Dad, Damon, Avi, Cassie, Daniel, Orion, and all my old friends from the Resistance. "I can't stop fighting. For... for their sakes. I can't give up."

The figure chuckled, then. As he did, the room lit up, and I saw my surroundings for the first time in God-knows-how-long. I was in some kind of dark cavern. It was massive. It stretched as tall as I could see, and the walls were further away than I could perceive. The sheer size of this place was enough to make the hairs on my arms stand on end, purely because something this big wasn't human. It wasn't man-made. It was alien. Totally alien.

The scariest thing about it, though?

That bright light, shining right in the middle of this cavernous void.

And yet...

"I can't give up," I said. "And I won't give up."

I held my breath and thought of all the pain in my life. As I thought of the pain—and there was a lot of it, not least the pain I'd felt these last few days, some of the purest pain of all—I felt my powers getting stronger once again. I could feel them charging up. I could feel the ice creeping down my spine, stretching down my arms, scaling my fingers, tickling my fingertips.

I went to lift my arms and fire at the one holding me.

Their grip around my neck loosened completely. I felt my

stomach turn as I dropped down below. Immediately, I triggered my flight powers, needing to regain some sense of composure.

But nothing happened.

I was still falling.

I felt my stomach drop as I hurtled toward the ground. I shouted out and lifted my hands in the air, trying to fire some kind of ice to the roof of this cavern.

But the cavern walls and ceilings were just too high.

The ice didn't grip with the walls.

I kept on falling.

As I fell, fear filling my body, scrambling from side to side, for a moment, I felt a sense of calm. It was weird and totally unexpected, but it was there.

Calm, because soon, there'd be nothing left of me.

Calm, because I wouldn't have to fight any longer.

And, ultimately, the position of not having to fight any longer was what I'd been striving toward all this time, right?

The cavern floor grew rapidly closer as I hurtled through the air toward it.

Sadness filled my body. I felt more tears roll down my cheeks, my throat wobbling. "I love you..." I started, intending to say "Mom" or "Dad" or "Ellicia" or anyone after it.

But in the end, there were so many people I loved that I couldn't say a thing.

I looked up. Above, I saw that total pitch black darkness again.

I felt the fear creeping up into my chest.

I held my breath.

Then, I fired one last shot of ice right up toward the ceiling.

I stopped.

Confusion filled my body. I spun left and right, still gasping in the darkness as I hovered there, totally static. *Did I do it? Did the ice stick?*

Then the face appeared in front of me all over again.

They were smiling, now.

Their smile made my body shake. I tried to look away, but I couldn't. It was like they had me wrapped up in some hypnotic trance.

They grabbed my neck again. I battled for that final breath. I didn't get a lungful.

"You should've given up when I gave you the opportunity," the voice said. "You were a fool for fighting. Now, we do things the hard way."

The figure stretched out their hand and pressed it against my chest.

Immediately, I felt a searing pain stretch through my body, and I lurched from side to side. "You won't win!" I shouted. "You'll never win!"

The figure smiled again, their hand still pressed against my chest. "That's where you're wrong, Kyle Peters. And this is where it ends for you, I'm afraid. It's been nice knowing you. But really, it's time."

The burning sensation in my chest spread right across my body. I tried to spark my powers, but the burning just seemed to melt my ice right away. I tried to teleport, but I couldn't. I was just too weak.

"You won't win," I shouted. "You won't..."

There was nothing else to say. I didn't even have the strength to speak now.

The figure pushed their hand further into my chest.

More pain.

More fear.

More weakness.

I saw a light blue glow illuminate in front of me, then. I felt sick right away. I knew what this was.

"You've already lost," the figure said, dragging the blue light from my body like they were taking away my innards. "Goodbye, Kyle Peters. Goodnight. This is where your story ends."

The last of the blue light was dragged from my body.

This is where your story ends...

I was starting to believe it, as my body gave up fighting, and darkness closed in.

[2]

I opened my eyes.

The light above me was bright, which made me squint right away, wishing I was back in the darkness that I'd been in for... hell. How long *had* I been in that darkness? And what even was that darkness?

All I knew was that something had happened. Something terrible.

The air was biting cold. It hit me like a punch to the gut, making me curl my arms over myself and hug my body in an attempt to heat myself up. Still, none of this made sense. Why was I here? Where was I? Why was I in the cold?

I blinked a few times, trying to get a sense of my surroundings. Everything was so bright. Snow covered the ground, and fell from the sky, too. By my side, there was a frozen lake, and something told me I'd *been* in that lake at some stage. I was all alone, wherever this was.

But the thing that bothered me and gnawed at my consciousness most was the dream.

I'd been in darkness. Total darkness. Someone had their

hands around my neck—or their claws, or whatever they were—and were tightening them. I remembered feeling in the dream like I understood why I was being attacked, and why everything seemed like it was falling apart. It'd felt so real.

But it wasn't real. *This* was real.

And *this* real sucked just as much as my dream reality.

The wind blew strongly against me, making my face even number than it already was. I rubbed at my cheeks to try and bring feeling to them, but that didn't do much good. My ears, which the wind howled past, were just as icy. So cold, in fact, that I could feel big icicles dangling from the ends of them.

Where was I?

What had I...

I saw it, then. I saw the events that had unfolded and led to me being stranded here.

I was fighting with Catalyst.

I'd fallen into the icy lake.

I'd held my breath as my life drifted away.

And then Catalyst had reached me, and...

Well, it was supposed to be the end. It was meant to be my big, great sacrifice.

But then I'd seen something else.

I'd woken up in some dark, alternate reality. Orion was there. As was Daniel Septer—my biological brother, also once known as Nycto.

Saint was also there. Saint, the great, villainous monster of a being who had reigned terror over the world for so many years.

Yet he was standing alongside Orion and Daniel, the pair of them facing the thing that was approaching.

I felt a deep sense of foreboding when I remembered what I'd seen. The hairs on my arms stood on end, and nausea climbed through my body.

I'd seen a great force approaching in the distance.

There was no other way of explaining what I'd seen. A *force*.

Only I knew, deep down, that force was heading toward Earth.

I looked up at the sky. Snow fell from above. The blue sky was peppered with clouds. I felt tension in my body, as I bit my lip, wondering whether that force I'd seen was out there, making its way rapidly toward me.

But hell. I had bigger problems on my plate right now.

Namely, being stuck in the middle of Antarctica, freezing my ass off, with no idea if what I'd seen was real or just a figment of my admittedly pretty active imagination.

I looked down at my hands. They were covered in ice. I needed to warm up, activating my powers—if I could find the strength.

I turned to a crouch, held my breath, and squeezed my eyes shut.

I pictured that force I'd seen.

The force that had Orion and Saint united, together, because whatever it was terrified them so much.

I saw it, and I felt a spark of warmth right in the middle of my chest, my powers getting close to the surface.

Then I felt that grip tighten around my throat, and I let go.

I collapsed to the ground. Icy snow covered my face, which made me feel even worse. I leaped back, swallowing a lump in my throat. I couldn't just give up here. I had to try again. I couldn't let my dreams get in the way.

I closed my eyes again, held my breath, and refocused my attention on something else.

My mom. The anger I felt about losing her.

But searching for that warmth in my chest was hard. I felt

like I was starting all over again, like all the practice I'd put into getting to the state I'd got to, power-wise, had been for nothing.

Still, I persevered. I was going to have to if I wanted to get out of here.

But what exactly was I going back *to*?

I'd defeated Catalyst, sure. But I knew I was the Failsafe he was looking for, now. The key that had the power to destroy all of humanity, if extracted in the right way.

And there was Ellicia, too. I'd seen what had happened to her. Part of the Failsafe was that it attacked those closest to me first, and Ellicia had fallen right in the firing line.

That gave me even more of a reason to get back home.

I gritted my teeth. I kept on pushing, trying to teleport back home with what little energy I had.

But those dreams—those things I'd seen—kept on returning to the forefront of my attentions, holding me back.

I gave up. I crouched there as the snow fell onto me, making me colder and colder by the second. I looked up into the sky and wondered, "What if?"

I had a decision to make.

Believe what I'd seen in my unconsciousness and face up to a terrifying reality—a reality that I honestly didn't think I was strong enough to face, not anymore.

Or dismiss them as what they seemed to be: dreams. After all, Orion was gone. So too were Saint and Daniel. I'd seen them in a near-death experience. My powers had somehow pulled me back out of that icy lake. Everything else was just fantasy.

I took a deep breath and cleared my throat.

In the end, there was only one option I was willing to believe.

I closed my eyes, gritted my teeth, and put all my energy into my thoughts of Ellicia.

This time, I slipped smoothly into teleportation mode, and drifted off into the unknown, back toward home.

I had to go back home.

And I had to go back to my normal life.

There was no point believing in fantasies.

But as I drifted through the tunnel home, I still couldn't shift those dreams from my mind...

[3]

When I got back home, I didn't exactly get the welcome I expected.

Snow was falling on the streets of Staten Island. I found that weird right away, as I swore when I'd left to fight Catalyst, it had been the end of summer—and a damned hot summer at that.

Other than the falling snow, there were other things that caught my attention, too. The billboards and posters attached to walls were advertising things I didn't recognize. The further I walked to my home, the more I triggered my invisibility because I didn't want to be seen. This whole place felt weird enough as it was. I wasn't sure I was ready to step back into it just yet.

There were the usual sounds of home that caught my attention, making me feel like I'd been away for a lot longer than I expected. The sound of traffic rushing by, and of horns honking right over on Manhattan Island. I could hear them right from over here. Yep, one of the annoying things about being a Staten Island resident—no matter how hard you tried, you couldn't escape the toxic buzz of the city.

The wind blew against me, and I immediately shivered,

covering my body with my hands instinctively. I still hadn't recovered from just how cold I'd been in Antarctica. I figured it'd take me a long while to recover, in truth.

But I just had to get back home. I had to know Damon, Ellicia, Avi, Cassie, and Dad were okay. I had to know.

Especially Ellicia.

I couldn't accept that she'd suffered the fate I thought she'd suffered when Catalyst triggered the Failsafe.

The closer I got to home, I smelled food coming from the takeaways. My stomach churned, and I turned my head to look at the curry houses and fried chicken places that I was so eager to indulge in. *No. There'll be time for that. You've got other things to do right now.*

I reached the front door of my home. I stood outside it, feeling somewhat nervous, preparing myself for what to say.

I walked over to the bell and went to press it.

The door opened before I could reach it.

Standing there, Ellicia.

I felt warmth cover me right away. Instinctively, my invisibility dropped. "El... Ellicia?"

I saw her dark hair shining in the glow of the hallway light. She looked... well, she looked older than she was when I'd last seen her. Not that much older, like she was suddenly forty-five or something, but she'd definitely aged.

But she was here.

She was alive.

Her eyes widened. Her jaw dropped. Her cheeks lost their color. "Kyle?"

My heart raced. I couldn't hold myself back anymore.

I stepped up toward her and wrapped my arms around her.

"Kyle," she said. I could hear she was crying now. "It is you. It really is you."

I pulled her closer. To be honest, she was doing a good job

of warming me up, but I didn't tell her that. Didn't exactly want to ruin the moment. "Of course it's me. I'm here. I'm here."

We held each other for a while. I kept my eyes closed. In that darkness, I saw the dreams replaying like they were biting at the outskirts of my consciousness.

But nothing could ruin this moment. Nothing.

"Kyle? Holy sh..."

I heard the voice, and I knew who it was right away.

When I lifted my head, I saw three people standing inside my house, right behind Ellicia.

Damon.

Avi.

Cassie.

"Jesus Christ, man," Damon said. "You're still here!"

The three of them piled around me, tightening their grip. As they did, I felt at ease in their embrace, just for a few seconds. But then the memories—the dreams—of having the life squeezed from me kicked in again, and I felt myself pushing them away. "Okay," I said. "It's cool. I'm fine. I just... I just need a little space to breathe. Please."

Damon had a wide grin on his face, which was even chubbier than I remembered. "Sure, man. Sure. Sorry. It's just... shit. You came back. You actually came back."

It seemed weird, standing here. Absurd, in fact. Something seemed weird about the way they were greeting me, almost as if they'd never been expecting to see me again. I scratched the back of my neck. "So, um... where's—"

"Come inside," Avi said. He pointed his thumb over his shoulder. "I mean, I don't really have to say that, seeing as it's your place and all. But seriously. Come in, boss. Welcome home."

I felt that weirdness all over again as I looked at each and every one of them.

The only person who hadn't said a word was my sister, Cassie.

She just looked at me with bloodshot, watery eyes, like she couldn't believe what she was seeing.

I took a deep breath and swallowed a lump in my throat. "Alright. Alright."

WE SAT around the table in my old kitchen. The kitchen had changed—a lot. There were whole new work surfaces fitted, a new fridge-freezer, and the table was long and rectangular now instead of flimsy and round. I realized right then that there clearly had been something weird going on for things to have changed so much. Just how long had I been in Antarctica?

"Dad moved out," Cassie said.

I narrowed my eyes. "He... he what?"

"He moved upstate. I still see him from time to time. But he likes his peace and quiet. He likes his fishing."

"And I don't blame him, man," Damon interrupted. "Should see the size of the fish that dude catches."

I heard more chatter and more laughs, but I couldn't get involved. It all seemed too much like everything was buzzing on around me at a million miles an hour.

"I think I'm going to see him on Friday," Cassie said. Then she looked down at her drink, which was half finished. "Or at least, I was."

I looked at her. Then I looked at Ellicia, Damon, and Avi. "What's happened? What's... what's changed?"

They knew what I meant. The things that had changed, and in such a short space of time.

"Kyle," Ellicia said. "The world. The whole world out there. They think you're dead."

I felt a tightness right in the middle of my chest. I reached for my glass of water, but I didn't sip any of it. "How... how do they—"

"The battle with Catalyst," Damon continued. "Which we won, by the way. The Resistance are still out there, but they've gone quiet, mostly because there's not been anything worth fighting lately. But the truth stands. The whole world thinks you sacrificed yourself to save the world."

I felt a bit queasy and lightheaded, so I stood up. I walked over to the window, looked outside.

"Maybe don't get too close, boss," Avi said. "Just in case, you know."

I heard him, but I couldn't act on what he'd said. All I could do was keep on looking outside. The world thought I was dead. So it didn't matter how much I wanted to return to life as normal—whatever normal was now. The world had changed, so I had to change with it.

"How long have I been out?" I asked.

There was no response. Just silence.

I turned around. "How long?"

Ellicia looked at me. "You've been away over a year, Kyle. And as far as the world's concerned, you've been dead for over a year."

I felt sick, right to the pit of my stomach. My face started to burn up. "I think I need to use the bathroom." I rushed across the room, toward the hallway.

On the way out, Avi stood. He patted me on the back, a sheepish grin on his face. "Happy nineteenth birthday, bruv."

I didn't feel much in the mood for celebrating.

[4]

I stared at myself in the mirror and wished myself a happy goddamned birthday.

It was night, and it was late. The bathroom was dark, illuminated only by the light I'd sparked in my palm. Outside, I could hear a couple shouting loudly at one another, fighting over whether he'd cheated on her first or the other way around, and how they were going to have to go on one of those TV talk shows to find out. I could still smell the takeaways, but they weren't even nearly alluring anymore, not after the discoveries I'd made. If anything, they brought a bitter taste to my mouth.

I'd missed a whole year of my life. Over a year, in fact. Eighteen months, as it turned out.

And now I was back and the world was getting on just fine, safe in the knowledge that I was dead.

I looked at the lines on my forehead, which I'd always had because I always had a look of surprise on my face, or so Mom used to tell me. Real great thing to tell a kid with self-esteem issues.

My hair was still the same length as it had been a year and a half ago. I didn't have any facial hair, dammit. In fact, I didn't look different at all.

It was as if I'd been in one of the cryogenic chambers or something, and now I'd woken up, while the world had continued around me.

I heard footsteps outside the bathroom, getting closer to the door. I didn't want to get caught or to speak to anyone, so I covered the light from my hand, closed my eyes and teleported myself back into bed. I didn't get into bed, though. I just sat there, listened to the bathroom door open, heard the footsteps creak along, heard the toilet flush. When everything had gone silent, I thought about going back to the bathroom, but instead, I stayed in my room. There was nothing else I had to see.

To be honest, I didn't so much want the company of anyone. I told them it was because I was tired. Really, it was because I was scared. I was trying to figure out and comprehend what I was dealing with, and still I couldn't be sure.

I walked over to my window and looked outside. The streets were quiet. The arguing couple wasn't arguing anymore. In fact, they were making out. I could hear the faint buzz from the nightclubs over on Manhattan, and I wished they'd go away so I could just stand in total silence for a while.

The thing that was bothering me more than anything?

I didn't want to go to sleep, because going to sleep meant facing the dreams.

I didn't want to face the dreams.

I walked over to my bed regardless, and sat on the end of it. I was exhausted, yawning uncontrollably. Whenever my eyes went to close, I jolted them right back open, my heart racing as I neared sleep.

I didn't want to see what I'd seen before I'd woken up in Antarctica. I didn't want to face that *force* that I knew was approaching Earth, because that force just felt too... well, real.

Yet how could it be?

How could it possibly be real?

I leaned back and stared up at the ceiling. I could see the little glowing stars that Dad had put there for me, as a throwback to my old room. The glow had faded on them, so I lifted my hand and sent a silvery light up toward them, restoring them to as good as new.

The things I'd seen and felt in the dreams couldn't be real, no. But neither could I have survived in Antarctica's freezing conditions, not a trace of me, for eighteen months, and then just return without so much as a scratch or a bit of stubble to show for it. Ellicia told me they'd been out to Antarctica, right to the scene of the fight, searching for me. They'd found Catalyst's body, frozen, and destroyed him for good. But they hadn't found me.

I lay still on my bed and listened to my churning stomach. As I lay there, I weighed up where I was at, and what I was going to do about it. I could believe what I saw in those dreams, and try to recreate them—try to figure out where Orion, Saint, and Daniel were, and stand by their side.

Or, I could close my eyes and believe they were just dreams, maybe even witnessing them all over again.

I swallowed a lump in my throat.

Believing they were reality was just too dangerous, as absurd a situation as this was.

I knew it was impossible that I was here and alive—and that I even had powers in the first place.

But I couldn't believe there was some *alien* force heading toward Earth. And that Orion, Saint, and Daniel were teaming up, let alone *alive* at all.

It was too far-fetched, in a world of farfetchedness.

I opened my eyes once more and looked up at those glowing

stars. They should've comforted me. Instead, they made my toes curl.

I lifted my hand and put out their glow.

And then I closed my eyes.

I was going to adapt to this new world in whatever way I could.

I was going to find a way to live a normal life, all over again.

Sleep crept up on me. I tried to keep my eyes wedged open, but it was too difficult.

In the end, I felt sleep wrapping its long, peaceful arms around me, and before I knew it, I was surrounded by the darkness, with nothing I could do about it...

[5]

It didn't take long for me to see death all around me.

The night was black and foreboding, but there was something different about it. It had a reddish glow to it. Either the glow of explosions or the glow of... something else. Something *worse.*

Large, heavy clumps of ash fell from above. Ahead of me, there were cities in ruin. Buildings burning. Skyscrapers collapsed. I saw it all playing out in front of me like I was moving from place to place. The Eiffel Tower collapsing. London Bridge snapped in two. Then closer to home, Central Park, up in flames, everyone running for their lives, the piercing screams making the hairs on the back of my neck stand on end.

I knew that everything around me was falling apart. I could see that everything was collapsing. And even though I couldn't identify or explain it, I knew *why* it was happening.

But more than that.

I knew my friends and my family were in danger.

I needed to help them.

I held my breath and flew across town, heading right for my house, where I hoped I'd find Cassie.

As I approached, I saw a massive chunk of debris falling from the sky, hurtling right toward me.

I didn't have time to think. I just swung to my right, hoping I could avoid its course before it could swat me out of the sky like a fly.

But the chunk of debris followed my turn and kept on pounding at me.

A surge of adrenaline shot through my body. I froze, caught in two minds: left or right, left or right?

In the end, I knew that left or right wasn't going to be enough.

I lifted my hands and fired a blast of ice at the debris.

The debris didn't break. In fact, it seemed like the collision with the ice only reinforced it, making it stronger, faster, more powerful.

My stomach sank. I did the only thing I could possibly do.

I flew away as fast as I could.

I looked down and saw my home. I knew Cassie would be in there. But I couldn't go inside. If I did, I'd be luring the debris to her. Yet I couldn't just fly away either, knowing what I knew, seeing the devastation all around.

I looked back, over my shoulder, to see how much time I had to attempt to rescue Cassie and the rest of my friends, Ellicia, everyone.

The debris wasn't alone anymore.

There were more chunks of debris. They were moving toward each other as if attracted by a magnetic force. And they were welding together, forming a huge, dagger-like object right above me.

My chest tightened. I knew that I was the only thing between this dagger and my home.

The dagger released, like an arrow, catapulting in my direction.

I lifted my hands and held my breath.

Then, I let out a cry.

Ice left my hands in thick, powerful streams.

I kept on pushing, kept on holding my breath, focusing all my attention on that oncoming dagger of debris.

The dagger slowed down when the ice hit it. It was still moving at me, though, just not hurtling as rapidly. I felt nausea building up. *It's going to break through. It's too strong for me.* I pushed back even harder.

The dagger of debris was so close to my face that I could almost feel it, now. And yet it wasn't what I expected. It wasn't sharp, heavy, painful.

It was like a tight grip around my chest.

Just like the dreams.

Just like the...

I blinked.

The dagger of debris was gone.

A shiver crept up my spine. I looked around. It had gone, completely.

But not just that.

The city, which had been under fire just seconds ago, was still. The buildings were destroyed. More ash clouds moved overhead, raining down. There was a total, echoey silence.

Everything beneath me was gone. Destroyed.

There was no trace of New York City. Just ash, dust, and bodies.

I looked away from the bodies and flew off into the distance. I couldn't look at the bodies. I couldn't allow myself to accept that this had happened. I'd tried to fight, but I wasn't strong enough. I knew it, and now the evidence of that truth was there for the world to see.

"Ellicia!" I shouted. "Damon! Cassie! Avi!"

All I got in response were echoes.

A spark ignited in my mind, then. Dad. He was upstate. He had to be safe up there. Maybe Ellicia, Damon, Cassie, and Avi were there with him, too. I don't know what made me think this. It might be nonsensical, but I was clinging to a nonsensical kind of hope now.

I started to fly off in the direction of upstate New York when I saw something behind me.

There was a darkness. A darkness so thick that it cut through everything else. It was moving slowly toward me, but fluidly. As it moved, it swallowed up everything around it—the shattered remains of cars, the broken up concrete, the fallen street lights.

As I looked at this darkness, I felt total fear. I was transfixed. Part of me wanted to stay and face it because I felt like I knew what was hiding behind it. I felt like I'd seen this happening all before.

But then I remembered Dad, and I knew I wasn't strong enough to face the darkness.

Instead, I had to run.

I shot myself upstate and landed on a farm. There were crops all around. They were still intact. So too was the farmhouse.

I hurried up the pathway, toward the steps. Everything was still very silent. Up above, the sky was turning a brown shade of gray. I swallowed a lump in my throat. I knew what it meant. The darkness was seeping in. I had to hurry.

"Dad?" I called, as I staggered up the steps.

The steps creaked under my feet. By the sides of the door, two plants, both totally withered.

The front door was ajar.

There were footsteps leading inside.

I felt my stomach sink. I stopped, looking at those footsteps.

Someone had got here before me. I had to hope it was someone good.

"Dad?" I called again. I walked past the plants, inside his home. I knew I'd never been here before, and yet it felt so familiar to me. Like I'd been here a thousand times.

The sofa was covered with a thick layer of dust. The television was smashed. The mirror had fallen and shattered everywhere, my jagged face reflected in the sharp shards.

My fear grew even more intense. "Dad? Please. Please..."

Then I stopped.

Dad was lying on the floor.

A shard of that mirror glass was poking out of his neck.

I felt the same way I'd felt when I saw the flames at my old house the night I'd lost Mom. I stumbled either side and then rushed over toward him.

"Dad. No. Ple—"

Then, I slipped into darkness.

I blinked a few times, and I realized right then that I was back.

The *force* was heading to me.

Orion, Saint, and Daniel were by my side.

Confusion taunted me. I looked from left to right, losing my grip on this reality. "This place. And—and my dad. What is it?"

Saint turned to me. "What you're seeing is what will happen if you don't believe."

I narrowed my eyes. "Believe what?"

Saint was silent, just for a few seconds. He turned back to look at the oncoming force. "You need to believe the world will collapse. You need to prepare for it. Or the world really will collapse."

I looked back at the force.

Only this time, I saw something in the darkness. Something

I could comprehend. But something I couldn't really understand.

There was a small, circular body of a creature. It looked metallic, like some kind of spaceship.

And shooting out of it were five long, metallic tentacles with pincers on the end, getting closer and closer and...

[6]

"Dad!"

I jolted upright. I was still surrounded by darkness, but this darkness wasn't as thick and foreboding as the darkness that had been in my visions.

No, not visions. *Dreams*. That's all they were.

Right?

A little moonlight peeked in through my window. It didn't make me feel much calmer, which I knew it should do, considering it confirmed that I *had* been dreaming again after all.

Instead, it just made me pull the bed covers over my head and squeeze my eyes tightly shut.

I wasn't sure how long I lay there, underneath the covers. I listened to the traffic passing by outside. I could hear birdsong, which meant daylight was approaching. My eyes kept on drifting shut, and I felt sickly and nauseous as hell through lack of decent sleep. But anything was better than those dreams. Anything was better than the destruction I'd seen, inside my mind.

I knew what I'd seen. I'd seen Orion, Saint, and Daniel there again. I'd been back in that awful place, wherever it was, that I'd gone to after I'd fought Catalyst. I'd seen something approaching. That dark *force* hurtling at me, all over again.

Only this time, I'd seen the face of that force.

I'd look deep into its eyes, and I'd seen the things surrounding it. The robotic creatures, with long, metal tentacular arms.

They were terrifying, but I'd seen what was beyond it, and although I knew I'd looked into the face of that oncoming darkness, I couldn't remember exactly what it'd looked like.

It was like my mind was forcing it out of the forefront of my consciousness, urging me not to see.

I heard footsteps creaking outside my room. Immediately, I tensed my fists. I would fight if I had to.

But then I heard Cassie's cough, as she walked down the stairs, clearly struggling for sleep just like I was.

I thought about going downstairs and joining her. I thought about telling her about the dreams. But I knew what that meant. Not only would Cassie take them seriously, goddammit, but *I'd* be forced to take them seriously too.

Taking the dreams seriously meant accepting that something really was wrong. That something was totally amiss.

I knew that Cassie and the others knew that there was something wrong about my disappearance, too. I'd told them I'd died. There was no way I could survive a thing like what happened to me.

And yet, somehow, I had, and I was here.

I pulled the covers away from my face and sat up at the end of my bed. I looked around my room. Television. PlayStation. Xbox. Laptop. All these things I used to distract myself with, and now none of them appealed at all.

I knew what my choices were. I either went downstairs and spoke to Cassie, or I didn't, and I kept on accepting that I was going to fall to sleep, and I was going to have those dreams.

I heard water pouring out of the tap, down into the sink.

There was still time to go down there and speak with my sister.

I heard her walking up the stairs, getting closer to her room again.

There was still time to go out. To face her.

I heard her stop just outside my bedroom door, and I wondered for a moment if she knew. If she wanted to speak just as much as I did. Maybe she was having the dreams, too.

I was just about to stand up and call her name when she kept on walking past my room and disappeared into her bedroom, and the moment was gone.

But the thoughts were not.

I couldn't face up to the dreams.

Something about them—something intangible, which I didn't even understand myself yet—was just too terrifying.

I put a little ice on the top and bottom of my eyelids and froze it solid enough to hold them in place.

I wasn't getting any sleep tonight.

[7]

"Shit, man. You look like crap."

I pulled my hood up, covering my face some more. I didn't want anyone to see me. As far as the world was concerned, I was dead, and I wanted to keep things that way. The second the world realized I was still alive again, they'd just find me another problem to solve. And I wasn't in the frame of mind to be solving problems right now.

It was a bright, crisp day. There was a lot of snow underfoot, which had frozen over. I had to watch my every step to make sure I didn't slide. If I did slide, I'd probably fall flat on my face. My hood would come back, and someone would see who I was.

Dammit. When would I start actually growing a decent amount of facial hair so I could hide my baby face for good?

The buildings of Staten Island towered over me. Okay, maybe not *Manhattan* towering, but towering enough to make me feel uncomfortable. I unzipped my coat a little at the neck and looked to my left, to my right, over my shoulder.

Then I felt a hand on my arm, and I flinched.

"Whoa," Damon said. He was walking with me, Avi by his

side. "Relax, man. It's Staten Island. No one's gonna see you, and no one's gonna care if they do."

I puffed out my lips. "No one will care?"

"Well," Damon said. "They'll care, sure. But what're you gonna do for the rest of your life? Keep your emo hood pulled up over your eyes and hope no one'll recognize you?"

I sighed. "Something like that."

We kept on walking along the sidewalk. There was more than one reason why I was keeping my hood up. I didn't want to be recognized, sure, but I also didn't want Damon or Avi or anyone, for that matter, to see how sleep-deprived I looked.

The dreams weren't far from my mind.

But hell. I'd made the decision to dismiss them. Now, I just had to try my best to live a normal life—as hard as that was going to be.

"Hell, hoods down after all," Avi said. "Some mean looking dudes up ahead."

I saw a trio of guys, probably a similar age to us, walking toward us, and my stomach sank. I reflexively pulled my hood down a little more and lowered my head a little.

The two guys on either side were muscular and well built, clearly overdoing it on the protein shakes. The one in the middle was small and weedy. I wondered whether they intentionally positioned themselves like that, to try and make it look like their leader had more weight and strength than it seemed.

It wasn't fooling me.

And yet still, I was scared.

"Hold up," the shorty in the middle said. He was sniffing at the air. "Is it just me or do I smell a bunch of dorks?"

His two friends chuckled. Right away, I felt my stomach sink some more. My instinct was just to keep on walking and stay out of trouble. Once upon a time, I might have tried to fight, but I just wanted to get on with spending some time with my friends. I didn't want any trouble today.

"Hey," a deep voice said. I felt a hand hit my chest, pushing me back. "I'm speaking to you."

I looked into the eyes of this short, scrawny little asshole, and I gritted my teeth together.

The scrawny kid lowered his head like he was trying to look into my eyes, underneath my hood. "Hullo? Is there a real life person in there?"

Again, his goofy friends chuckled. Surprised if they had a brain cell between them.

"You should back off," Damon said.

All of them turned to him and narrowed their eyes.

"What did you just say?"

"I said you should back off."

Silence followed. My heart pounded. I didn't want any trouble. I just wanted Damon to stop.

"Hold on," the short guy said, raising his hands. "I recognize you."

My heart leapt. For a second, I thought he was speaking to me.

But then I realized his eyes were squarely focused on Damon.

"Yeah, you're familiar. You're... Shit. You're one of those freaks, aren't you? The freaks with the powers? Holy hell, Seb! It's one of those freaks!"

I heard their laughter and their amazement, and I felt a different emotion. This time, I felt total disgust. Disgust that these people were mocking my best friend, laughing off his abilities like he hadn't done anything bold or grand like, oh, I dunno, saving the whole damned world.

"You should show some respect, boss," Avi mumbled.

In my mind, I was begging him just to stop.

The trio turned their attention to Avi. They looked him up and down, a glimmer of disgust in the short guy's eyes. "And why would I do that?"

"Because these guys saved your lives. They saved all your lives."

There was a pause.

Then, the short guy turned to me. "These *guys*?"

My body went cold. I felt my muscles tightening. "Come on," I said, grabbing Damon and Avi's arms. "Let's—"

"No," the short guy said. As he spoke, the two muscular guys beside him grabbed me by the biceps, holding me in place. "You don't go anywhere. Not without telling us your name."

Total fear washed over me. I could feel my skin crawling, my cheeks going pale. I looked at Damon and then at Avi, but I knew I was alone in this. This problem was mine to deal with. I just wasn't sure if I had the strength to.

"Let's see your face," the short guy said. He nodded at his friend on the right.

The guy pulled up my hood.

I held my breath.

There were two things that happened, then. On one hand, I saw the swift recognition in the eyes of all three of these guys. I saw them looking at me like they knew me, and then realizing *how* they knew me.

I should've been afraid. I should've been goddamned terrified.

I didn't have a chance to be.

Because behind the trio we were standing off against, there was a blast.

It was loud, and it shook the ground beneath. Right away, a ball of fire rose from the crash site, illuminating the sky a weird shade of red.

There was a darkness there, too. A thick blackness that made me wonder, what if?

"Shit," the short guy said, his voice cracking. "Let's—let's get the hell out of here."

They ran away as the screams and the shouts started to rise around the crash site.

I heard Damon saying things to me.

I heard Avi saying things to me.

But all I could focus on was what I was seeing.

The thing that had caused the explosion had fallen from the sky.

The thing that had caused the explosion was one of those machines I'd seen in my dreams.

The metallic object with long, sharp tentacles by its side.

And following it, darkening the sky, there was another one, just like it.

"What do we..." Avi started.

But it was too late.

Before the thing could crash into the earth and crush us in its path, I grabbed the pair of them and teleported them away.

But even as I disappeared, I knew what was happening, and what I had to face up to.

My dreams were coming true.

They were a reality after all.

[8]

"Kyle, what is it? Because something's on your mind. I can just tell."

I heard Ellicia's voice, but I couldn't respond to her words. I was sat on her sofa, holding her hand. The television was on; the volume turned up to the max. Every channel was filled with the same news report: the strange object that had crashed into earth in New York. The devastation it had caused.

There were all kinds of speculation. Talks that this was an alien invasion. There were reports that this was some kind of fallen satellite. There were even rumors of government experiments, and some talk of ULTRAs.

But really, nobody knew. And that's what stirred up the fear more than anything.

"Kyle?" Ellicia said, squeezing my hand. "What's wrong?"

I swallowed a lump in my dry throat. My eyes stung, my body crying out for sleep but my mind begging for anything but. I turned and looked at Ellicia; the first time I'd looked away from the television all afternoon. "It's just... this. It's pretty scary. Don't you think?"

Ellicia narrowed her eyes. "I know when you're lying to me, Kyle. You're hiding something from me. What is it?"

I turned away and sighed. I should've known better than to lie to Ellicia. She was becoming almost as good as my sister at telling when I wasn't being completely honest.

"I mean, you come back here out of nowhere. And all of a sudden you're acting all weird. You clearly haven't been sleeping. The whole world thinks you're dead and now..." She pointed at the television, the rolling news of the devastation caused by the fallen craft. "Now this. What's happening, Kyle? And don't tell me you're just interested in this because you think it's a little weird."

I lowered my head. I knew I had a choice. I could tell Ellicia what I'd seen in the dreams, or I could keep those dreams to myself. Neither choice was easy. If I told Ellicia, again, it was the same-old problem of facing up to a problem I wasn't sure I was strong enough to fight. If I kept it to myself and things got worse, I was going to be forced to live with the knowledge that I could have done something to prevent it; I could have acted.

But could I?

What was I supposed to do?

Outside, I heard sirens, which just made me feel sick because they reminded me just how close the chaos really was. I looked back at the screen, where various news reporters from around the world were all talking and discussing this craft.

"We've got sources in China suggesting that this really could be some kind of intergalactic threat."

And another report: "It's clearly a satellite. You can tell from the antenna that it's a satellite."

And another: "What if this is Saint? What if there's someone out there—someone worse than Saint—and who is here to defend us now?"

I heard all the panic, all the confusion, and I knew that I was doing the world a disservice if I just sat back.

"If you know something," Ellicia said, "then you have a right to do something about it. I know you might not like the sound of that, but it's who you are. You're Kyle Peters. You're Glacies."

I felt my toes curl when Ellicia said my name, and the word "Glacies." That name didn't have the might that it used to have, at least not in my mind. Because Glacies was me, and I wasn't strong enough.

But she was right. I did have a right to do something about it. I had a duty, even.

I put my arm around Ellicia and I pulled her close. "I'm gonna be okay. *We're* gonna be okay."

She moved in closer to me. "I hope so, Kyle. I really do."

Ellicia fell asleep on my shoulder. I kept my focus on the television.

But when she was snoring, I gently moved her aside, resting her head on the pillow.

The police might have set up a perimeter around the fallen object.

The army might be securing the area.

But I had to know what was happening because it felt to me like something terrible was unfolding.

I stood up, took a deep breath, and looked down at Ellicia.

Then I closed my eyes, gritted my teeth together, and teleported out of here.

I didn't want to face up to what I'd seen in those dreams.

But I was going to that fallen object, whatever it was.

I was going to find out what it was doing here.

[9]

I hovered above the crash site and waited for the perfect opportunity.

The moon shone brightly in the night sky. There was a chill in the air, as Christmas fast approached. I knew more snow would be on its way. The snow always hit New York hard, causing havoc and chaos for residents and tourists alike. Had to admit, it was kinda funny how much havoc it caused tourists as soon as they realized "New York snow" wasn't the romantic thing the movies and television shows made it out to be.

But this year, I figured there'd be way more focus on some other object that'd fallen from the sky than a bit of snow.

The crash site was just as weird and as amazing as I'd expected. There was a crater, that must've been about fifty meters deep. Protruding from that crater, a perfectly spherical dark metallic object. By its side, there were long, metallic arms, like tentacles, with pincers on the end. The first one of those objects that'd fallen was smaller, but this was massive. A pincer alone was enough to pick a person up and throw them right across the New York skyline.

I was afraid of this situation. Of course I was. Who wouldn't be? But I was Glacies. And I knew that meant I had a duty to the whole world to investigate this craft, if that was indeed what it was after all.

I ignored the fact that I'd seen this craft before, in what I believed were my dreams. I didn't know what to make of those visions.

I just knew that right now, I had to get on with investigating, for the good of myself and the good of everyone else.

There was a line of armed guards standing in front of the crash site. They were wearing military gear and were armed to the brink. Beside them, there were water cannons, as journalists scrambled around them. There was another line further in front of them, too—a line of police officers, who were trying to calm people down.

I felt a twinge of nervousness in my stomach as I made sure my invisibility was triggered. I knew I was going to have to be careful. These guys were armed to the max, and they didn't look like they were messing around.

I drifted down toward the craft, keeping my movement and my focus steady. I couldn't afford to make any mistakes. If I could just teleport inside that craft, I would, but I didn't know a thing about it so I had to make sure I was staying as safe as I could.

That didn't make me a pussy. It just made me *not* reckless. There was no room for recklessness.

I floated directly above the craft. Down inside it, I could see an opening right on top. That opening led down to even more darkness. There were forensics looking around it, but it didn't look like anyone had gone in there yet.

I swore I could hear something coming from that opening. Something droning. Like a heartbeat.

I swallowed a lump in my throat and moved slowly down toward the opening.

When I was just ten meters away, a crackle of electricity sparked right in front of me.

The burning pain split through my body. I jolted back immediately. Damnit. There was some kind of force field erected over the crash site, probably by the army. Of course there was.

The guards turned around and looked in my direction, not directly *at* me but through me.

They lifted their guns.

And they fired.

I covered my face as the bullets peppered toward me. I jolted from left to right, clinging on to my invisibility, in no real direction, just pure reflexive reaction.

I kept on moving as more bullets fired at me. I knew I wasn't going to be able to easily get through that force field. I was going to have to try something else.

I closed my eyes and dropped down to ground level. The guards were still firing above. Hope sparked inside me. That was a good thing. They couldn't see me. The invisibility had worked just fine.

I took a few deep breaths, standing right before the guards now. My heart pounded. If my invisibility dropped just for a second, they'd see exactly who I was, and the secret would be out.

Sure, those three idiots had seen my face not long ago. But I figured they'd have put me to the backs of their minds now a goddamned alien craft had fallen from the sky.

I studied my surroundings. The army dudes were right in front of me. The police and the crowds, behind me. I was sandwiched in the middle of them.

But beyond the army, there were forensics people. So there had to be some kind of opening through this force field.

I waited, as painful as waiting was. Every second that

passed, I became more and more paranoid that something was going to go wrong.

I had to wait, though. I had to see how they'd got inside.

I must've been standing there in silence for a whole fifteen minutes before I saw one of the forensics lift a hand and press it against what looked like thin air.

My body tensed. I immediately shot myself over there, so I was right in front of him.

As his hand was raised, I could see the force field peeling away, one piece at a time.

I held my breath.

This was my moment.

This was my chance.

The second the forensics guy stepped through in my direction... I moved right through him.

He staggered either side. He looked around.

"Jim?" someone to his side asked. "You okay?"

Jim scratched the back of his neck. "Yeah. Uh. I just felt, uh. A little light-headed, that's all."

I moved to the opening quickly now. The craft was even more fascinating and even more foreboding now I was standing right on it. It felt softer on my feet than I'd expected. Sure, it looked cold and metal, but there was a weird warmth to it. A warmth that felt like home.

I looked down into the opening. The hairs on the back of my neck stood on end.

I had to go in there.

It was my duty.

I closed my eyes, held my breath, and I dropped right down.

When I landed inside, what I saw wasn't exactly what I expected.

I'd pictured, in my mind, a wide open area, something

unlike anything I'd ever seen. Some kind of fascinating alien structure.

Instead, I just saw walls of wires. Little flashing lights. Like this was all some kind of computer system. A very human looking computer system.

I walked slowly down the corridor. My heart raced at a million beats per second, or at least in that region. The wires and the lights were all different sizes, all different colors. It struck me, as I followed the narrow corridors of this craft, that it really was what I called it—a *craft*. It had been crafted by someone.

I heard something behind me.

A rustling noise. Like little metallic footsteps.

I turned around.

There was nothing there.

I swallowed a lump in my throat. I had to keep going and see more of this craft. I was imagining the sounds. It was probably just the noise from above reverberating down here.

I turned back around and stepped further down this tunnel.

As I got further inside, it started to narrow. I felt the wires brushing against my face, snakelike in their texture.

Then I heard the rustling behind me again.

I spun around, faster this time.

And this time, I saw something.

It was only for a split second, but there was definitely something there. Minuscule yellow eyes watching me through the wires.

I was so focused on those eyes that I didn't see the other eyes right behind me.

I didn't even clock the being as it punched me hard in the back of my head, smacking me down to the solid floor beneath, the metal echoing as I slammed against it.

I felt dizzy and dazed. I tried to turn around. What had happened? What had punched me?

I didn't have to wait long to find out.

When I turned onto my back, I saw it.

There was a spherical thing right opposite me, with long tentacular arms. It was just like the craft I was inside, only smaller, just a little taller than me.

It pulled back its tentacle and went to slam it into my head.

Total fear overcame me. I stuck my hands out to cover my face, but none of my powers sparked. I was trapped; this was it.

I felt the tentacle hurtle into my body, and for a moment, I thought it was over.

That's when I felt someone grab me from behind.

And then I felt myself being hurtled through a wormhole, teleported away from those crafts, far away from the crash site.

When I fell through the wormhole, I opened my eyes right away. I was in some kind of disused office block, a few stories off the ground. In the distance, I could see the lights, where I knew the crash site was.

"You're an idiot for going in there alone," a voice said. "But at least you're willing to accept what's real, now."

My insides turned to mush.

My jaw tightened.

The man standing over me wasn't just anyone.

It was Saint.

[10]

"You don't have to look at me with such distrust anymore, Kyle. You and I are on the same side now."

I had to admit, accepting I was on the same side as the dude who'd nearly obliterated the planet, and who hated humans with a passion—and *me* even more—was kinda hard to accept.

It was dark outside, right in the middle of the night. I was in a disused office block type thing that was run down and full of dust. There were stacks of paper and broken old office equipment that looked like it'd been in here for a long time, but like the place had just been abandoned for no real reason. It was strange, for sure.

The strangest thing, of course, was Saint, who stood over me.

I had to keep on glancing up at him to check it was really him. Whenever I heard his voice, I flinched. I wondered if he knew that, and he was getting some kind of deranged pleasure out of how baffled I was by everything. I hadn't spoken a word yet. My mouth was too dry; my lips were too sore.

"You're probably wondering why I'm back here. How I got back here. Well, mostly, that's thanks to you."

He turned and smiled at me. He wasn't masked, revealing his pale, scarred face.

My skin crawled.

"The wormhole you sent me into was pretty much impenetrable to any ULTRA of Earth's current capacity, granted. And that's a credit to your abilities. But what you didn't stop to consider was that it might not be impenetrable to... something else."

"What is that thing?" I asked.

"Ahh," Saint said. "He speaks."

"No bullshit. Just tell me what's happening here."

Saint walked over to me. He stood right over me. For a few seconds, I actually felt afraid of his presence, recoiling a little. Then I remembered I'd beat him already, so there was nothing to fear.

Right?

"We don't understand what it is. Not truly. But we do know it's come from... from somewhere else. And we do know it's exploited the wormholes you created as a means to get here. So congratulations, 'Glacies'. You led it right here."

He turned around and walked away. I couldn't believe what he was saying. *I'd* brought that thing here? "What does it mean?"

Saint stopped. He was standing right in front of the door. He didn't respond, not for a few seconds. Then he looked over his shoulder and faced me. "I guess we'll have to find out for ourselves, won't we?"

He opened the door.

"Who's we?"

Saint didn't have to answer.

When he opened the door, I saw Orion and Daniel standing side by side.

Orion didn't have his mask on, but I recognized him from the time he'd showed me his face. Daniel wasn't masked either. He was paler, and he looked malnourished, but it was him. It was definitely him.

I felt a surge of both relief and also pain that I'd thought these two were gone.

I hurried toward them.

Without being able to stop myself, I wrapped my arms around Orion and held him tight.

"I thought you were gone," I said.

"Kyle," Orion said. He patted me on the back of my head, like he was uncomfortable in the embrace.

"I thought—I thought you were gone. Both of you."

Daniel half-smiled and nodded. "I guess you always were the emotional one, huh?"

We held each other a little longer, and I saw then that the dream I'd had was real. There was no other way about it. That hurt, in a way. Obviously, it was great, because it meant that Orion and Daniel weren't dead.

But it also meant that Saint wasn't dead.

And that meant that something terrible really was happening here.

"I'm all for grand emotional reunions," Saint said. "Really, I am. But you have a decision to make, Kyle. You have a reality to face up to."

My adrenaline dropped. I stepped away from Orion. "What decision?"

"You join us. And we get the Resistance—every single ULTRA left—together. We take the fight to the oncoming force."

"The oncoming force?"

"You've seen it," Daniel said. "Don't play dumb."

I lowered my head. "I had a nightmare. That's... that's all it was."

"Or," Saint said, dismissing my words. "You walk away and watch the world crumble."

I frowned. I still couldn't believe what Saint was saying. More than that, it didn't sit right that Saint was giving the orders. "You killed... you killed Orion. My dad. And then you expect us just to follow you?"

"Erm. In case you haven't noticed, your father is standing right here."

I could barely look at Orion or anyone but Saint anymore. "No. This is wrong. Something's... something's not right here."

"Believe whatever you want to believe," Orion said, speaking in his deep, to-the-point voice. "But... differences aside, Saint is right."

My jaw dropped. I looked between Saint, Orion, and Daniel, awestruck.

"We come together. Or the world falls. It's as simple as that."

Part of me wanted to believe these three. But something was wrong. There was a look in Orion's eye, and in Daniel's eye, that made me wonder if this was all some kind of illusion. Maybe it was Saint pulling the strings.

Or maybe it was something else...

"No," I said.

Orion frowned. "What—"

"I said no."

"You can't just—"

But I didn't stop around to hear what else Orion had to say.

I took a deep breath, closed my eyes and vanished.

This wasn't my battle.

This wasn't my fight.

Saint, Orion, and Daniel stood together in that disused, abandoned office block.

"Should we go after him?" Daniel asked.

Saint took a deep breath and sighed. "He'll come back. As soon as he realizes what a grave mistake he's making."

"And if he doesn't?"

Saint looked right at Daniel. "Then God help us all."

[11]

I didn't want to think about what I was doing. I just knew there was no other option.

I had to get away from the crash site, and I had to get Ellicia, Damon, Cassie, and Avi as far away from that crash site as possible.

I shot through the night sky back toward my place, where I knew Cassie and Ellicia were staying. The rain was falling heavily now. In a way, it felt warmer than it usually did, which only went to make me wonder even more. Was the warmth something to do with the craft—or the being, or *whatever* it was—that had fallen from above? Possibly. Was I reading into this stuff way too much, giving it more credit than it was worth? Probably.

Whatever. I had to get Ellicia and Cassie away from here. Then I had to get Damon and Avi away, too.

I opened my eyes as I teleported myself back inside my home.

But something happened.

I wasn't back inside my home at all.

I was on the street outside, lying flat on the ground.

I scrambled to my feet and looked around. What was I doing lying down in the road? Was I so rusty and out of practice that I couldn't teleport effectively anymore? No. That couldn't be the case. I'd teleported a few times since getting back to reality. I'd even managed to teleport myself from the Antarctic wastelands back to New York. It had to be something else.

I looked around. It felt like there was something pulling at me, a force from above dragging me out of place.

I shook my head. "Whatever. Damned excuses."

Then I went to teleport myself inside my home.

A splitting headache pierced through my skull. I fell to my knees, the rain splashing up against me. I could taste blood on my lips, as the sounds of honking horns nearby were louder and more pronounced than I knew they were in reality.

"What the hell?"

The pain was still intense, but it was better now I'd stopped trying to teleport. It still felt like there was something above me, affecting my current, like some kind of weird, draining magnet.

Whatever it was, I didn't like it. I wasn't going to play nice with it if it wasn't going to play nice with me.

I decided against teleporting inside my home and opted for the more human approach of taking the stairs.

I ran up the stairs. But the higher I got, I felt the breath beginning to drift from my body, the steps getting more and more cumbersome. I didn't want to slow down, but I found myself falling before I had a say in the matter. I put my head in my hands and panted for air. What was happening to me?

I tried to keep on moving, keep on climbing. The tiredness and the fatigue weren't easing. Maybe it was something to do with how long I'd been out cold. Perhaps it had affected me in many more ways than I could've imagined, and only now was it truly catching up with me.

Or maybe it was something to do with the fallen craft.

I swallowed a lump in my throat when I thought of the craft.

I didn't want to believe it was as much as a threat as Saint—if it even was Saint at all—claimed it to be.

Yet at the same time, I didn't want anyone I cared about being anywhere near it when shit went down.

I forced my way to the top of the stairs and reached Cassie's door.

"Kyle?"

I turned around and saw Ellicia frowning at me.

"What... Are you okay?"

She hurried over to me, her steps gradually picking up in pace.

"It's okay," I said. "I'm okay."

"You don't look okay. Cassie? I think we need to call an ambulance."

"No, wait—"

"Cassie!"

It didn't take long for Cassie to get to Ellicia's side. And when she got there, I heard Ellicia saying things, mumbling things about how she needed to go and get help, and I wanted to intervene and stop her, but I was just too weak. The pressure in my head was intense, like someone was squeezing either side of my temple, the juices inside my skull on the verge of bursting out.

And then in my blurred vision, I saw Ellicia leave, and I was alone with Cassie.

Cassie and the Force.

The Darkness.

The...

No. What was I thinking?

I felt something crack across my face, then. A sharp slap. Cassie's backhand.

"Hey," she said. "Bro? You need to pull yourself together."

"I can't exactly pull myself together when..."

I realized something weird had happened, then.

I had my strength and my energy back. In fact, it was as if I hadn't even lost it at all.

I stood up and walked over to the other side of the room, over to the door that Ellicia had left through.

"Um, Kyle?" Cassie said. "What the hell do you think you're doing?"

"Ellicia," I said. "I need to go get her. We—we need to get out of here."

"You're supposed to be having some kind of weird seizure on the floor."

"I feel better now."

"You feel better? Kyle, what's going on?"

I knew I wasn't going to get away from Cassie's grilling anymore. She was good at telling whether I was lying, so it was better just not even attempting to cover up the truth. "It's... it's this craft. This thing that's fallen from the sky."

"It's weird, I know. Doesn't take a genius to see something's off about it."

"Saint's back," I said.

There was a pause, then. I saw the shock on Cassie's face. She turned pale, opened her mouth, then closed it again. "He's... How's he..."

"All I know is he's back, and he's brought Orion and Daniel with him."

Cassie's face went even paler. "And you're only just telling me this now?"

"Look. I struggled believing it myself. But Saint insists that something's happening with this craft. That somehow, someone from outside of this planet found a way to intercept our wormholes and attack Earth. I know. It's weird. It's absurd. I'm not sure if I believe it or not either. And I sure as hell know I can't do a thing about some intergalactic threat. But I can get you and Ellicia and Damon and Avi as far away from here as possible. I just need to find them."

There was a look on Cassie's face then. It didn't take me long to register that it was disappointment.

"You knew," she said.

Shame crept into my body. I felt my cheeks turning red. "I didn't—"

"You knew, and you kept it from us. You knew something was wrong, and you ignored it."

"I didn't ignore it."

"You're a coward, Kyle."

That word pierced me like a sword to the gut. "What?"

Cassie was crying now. "You're a coward. Since you got back, I can tell you're afraid. Like you've regressed. It's almost like you—"

"Like what?" I shouted. "Like I don't want to be a freak anymore? Like I don't want to be the world's damned savior every time it needs one? Like I don't want to *die*?"

My voice echoed against the walls. I knew right away I shouldn't have shouted.

"I'm sorry," I said.

Cassie didn't even flinch. "And I'm sorry too. For whatever happened to you in Antarctica. But what you're doing now? Quitting? Giving up? That's shitty."

She turned around and walked away.

"Cassie," I said.

"I'm getting my gear, and I'm getting ready to do what I have to do. Even if you aren't going to be by my side. I'm not letting you hold me back. Not again."

I didn't want to let her go. I was so close to doing.

But then the lights flickered, and everything went black.

I stood in total silence for a while. The nerves built up inside. "Cassie?"

"I'm here. What's... Blackout or something?"

But as I walked to the window, I realized it wasn't a power cut at all. Not any ordinary power cut, anyway.

The world outside the window was pitch black. Every light, every car, everything electrical had come to a stop.

There was total blackness.

The only thing I could see made me want to puke.

It made every muscle in my body tighten to the point of no return.

"What is that?" Cassie asked, standing by my side, staring out the window.

I looked up at the large, dark object hovering over the pitch black planet, and I cleared my dry throat. "It's them," I said.

"Who?"

"The ones Saint warned me about. The one in my dreams. They're... they're here."

[12]

I stared out of the window and watched as the mothership—if that's indeed what it was—hovered above Earth.

It might be totally dark outside, but this mothership was even darker, a thicker black than the rest of the surroundings, making the night sky seem like daylight in comparison. There was a total silence to New York City that was eerie, like everyone here was watching. Of course, the whole world wouldn't be watching, because something had happened to the power when this obelisk of a structure arrived. It'd cut out, presumably leaving everywhere in the dark as to what was going on in this city. Maybe the whole world was even plunged into darkness, too.

Cassie was by my side, but she might as well have not been, and I might as well not be here either. We were both transfixed by this thing. We'd seen a lot of things in our lives. All sorts of remarkable, unbelievable things that previous generations would dismiss as science-fiction.

This was real.

The mothership was enormous. It was perfectly smooth. A low hum seemed to radiate from it, which made my stomach turn. There were things around it, too. Smaller ships, I realized, much like the crafts that had crash-landed into New York.

So they really were just crafts, here to accompany the real thing.

I stared closely at the mothership and somehow, I thought I could see something familiar right in its midst. Like piercing eyes staring back at me.

"What... what is..." Cassie started.

She didn't finish, because an enormous screech blasted out of the mothership. I clenched my teeth together, fell to the floor. My head was spinning. It felt like this screech really gnawed at the core of my abilities.

Then, a few seconds later, right in my mind, I heard a voice.

"People of Earth. ULTRAs of Earth. You don't know who we are and you do not need to know. All that you need to know is that you have to cooperate."

The voice was deep. Male. It sounded both alien and familiar, both at the same time.

I turned to Cassie. "You hearing this?"

She didn't have to answer to give me her response.

The voice continued, "The ULTRAs of this planet will tear you apart. You might believe that the threat has subsided; you might think that you are comfortable, and you might be able to sleep at night. But you cannot. Because they are still out there, and they will destroy this world. That's why you have to let us do our work, even if it means a few sacrifices along the way."

My guts turned to mush. I looked at Cassie, and she looked back at me, fear on her face.

"So now you must understand something. This world is ours, while we do our job. If you allow us to do our job, without resistance, you will be rewarded. If you do not..."

The voice didn't finish. It drifted off into the distance. But it was even more foreboding by the fact that it didn't finish.

"Allow us to do our work. Hand over your ULTRAs. Otherwise, we will find them. Because if we don't, they will destroy you. They will destroy all of you."

The voice disappeared, like a popping in my ears. I felt pretty sick. I took a few deep breaths, steadied myself, then I stood back up, light-headed.

I stood up and looked at Cassie. She stood up too, clearly not at ease.

"Now you have to make the call," she said. "You have to be strong. You see that, don't you?"

I swallowed a lump in my throat. I didn't want to have to face up to reality, but I could see reality in front of me, like a fork in the road: either I continued trying to deny what was happening, or I faced up to it.

I couldn't just deny what was happening.

As Kyle, I wasn't strong enough. I was going to have to be Glacies if I wanted to survive, let alone win.

But I was going to need some help.

"Yeah," I said. "I guess. But we're gonna need some help."

Cassie nodded. "I know where we can find Vortex, and—"

"But first, I need to get to Ellicia. I need to make sure she's safe."

Cassie sighed, then nodded. "Yeah. Of course. Right. Let's go get her."

I looked out of the window and saw the tentacled crafts hovering around, preparing to launch their reign of terror on the world.

"I'm coming for you, Ellicia," I muttered. "I'm coming."

[13]

I held Cassie's hand tightly and teleported us over to Ellicia's place.

But again, something was wrong.

And that something was me, lying on the ground outside, back aching after slamming into it.

My teleportation had failed again.

I rubbed the top of my head and winced, trying to reorient myself. I could taste blood again right at the back of my throat, and there was a strong metallic smell in the air. Out in the darkness, everything somehow managed to seem even darker than it had when I was looking out at it, if that was at all possible.

I was nervous, of course I was. I couldn't help it.

But nothing was going to stop me getting to Ellicia and making sure she was safe.

Not this darkness.

Not whatever the enemy had to throw at me.

Not even my dodgy teleportation.

Nothing.

"So, how long's your teleportation been playing up?" Cassie asked.

I steadied myself to my feet. "Since the aliens showed up, pretty much."

"You really think that?"

"Think what?"

"That they're aliens."

I paused for a few seconds. "I don't really know. But it doesn't matter who they are. We've got to—"

"Get to Ellicia. Right. Got it. After you, Mister Dodgy-Teleportation."

I felt diminished when Cassie mocked me like that. Like I was more Kyle Peters than I was Glacies. The enemy must be hampering my abilities somehow. For all I knew, I was sending a signal of my location right to them just by using my powers.

"You ready?" I asked.

Cassie nodded. "Ready."

Nervousness crept in as I closed my eyes, held my breath and thought of all the bad things that had happened in the last few years.

The deaths.

The destruction.

All of it...

I felt that energy burning in my chest, building up, and a part of me wanted to resist it.

Instead, I let it flourish.

Then I blasted it out in front of me and teleported myself over to Ellicia's.

We landed in an even darker alleyway. I could hear footsteps somewhere behind me.

"Is this Ellicia's?" Cassie asked.

Truth be told, I wasn't sure if it was Ellicia's. It was too dark even to get my bearings. There wasn't much moonlight or starlight anymore, not now the massive craft that the enemy had arrived on was blotting out the sky.

"I don't know," I said.

Cassie snorted. "You don't know?"

"Why's that so wrong?"

"Oh, no reason at all. Just expected you to know where your girlfriend lives, that's all."

"Look, if you don't want to be here, you don't have to be. I've got this, Cassie. Okay?"

There was no response.

"Cassie?"

I turned around slowly.

Cassie was staring right at me. Of the low level of night vision I was using, I could see that her eyes were wide.

Something had her attention. Something... terrifying.

I heard footsteps, then. Rustling, right behind me.

I swallowed a lump in my throat as that rustling got louder.

Don't turn around. Don't turn around.

But I had to.

I turned.

There was a large, circular being opposite me. It was standing on two metal tentacles, for legs.

Two more of those tentacles were sprouting from its side.

"Kyle, watch—!"

I didn't hear the rest of what Cassie said because the tentacle smacked me right across the face.

I hit the floor with a heavy thud. I tasted blood. All sounds and senses were muffled.

I opened my eyes and tensed my fists. I could hear Cassie shouting things, and the blast of her purple electricity hitting the being that had knocked me down.

I tried to pull myself up and fight.

Then another knock smacked me in the head.

My vision distorted even more than it already had. As I lay there on the ground, I couldn't deny feeling weak. I wasn't

Glacies anymore. Whether I liked it or not, I was Kyle Peters, and Kyle Peters wasn't as adept to fighting enemies as Glacies was.

Then I heard a yelp.

Right away, my stomach sank. I tightened my fists. That yelp. It was Cassie's.

I clenched my jaw and held my breath.

I bounced up to my feet. My hands were covered in ice. My heart was racing, and sustaining my powers felt far, far harder than it ever used to.

But I was standing, and I had my powers activated.

That counted for something.

The craft was standing over Cassie. Cassie was on her back. The tentacle was getting ready to hurtle into her.

"Hey," I said.

The craft turned around, human-like in its movement.

"Be careful who you screw with," I said.

The craft swung a tentacle at me, fast and hard.

This time, it didn't hit me.

I stopped it before it reached my face, using my powers of telekinesis.

I twisted it around so that it started curving away from me, pointing right at the craft.

The craft kicked back with another tentacle, trying to knock me off my feet.

I hopped up instinctively, then I grabbed that tentacle with my icy hand and started to freeze it, the metal sizzling as I poured more and more power into my resistance.

Behind the craft, I saw Cassie standing. The purple electricity was charged up in her hands. I felt a twinge of adrenaline. We were doing this, together. We were taking this monster down.

And then I slipped and fell back once again.

All the ground I'd made felt like it slipped away in that instant.

The craft was over me.

All its tentacles were free of my grip and raised right above my head.

I looked into its shiny metal body and waited for the arms to hit me.

Then electricity sparked all over the craft.

I scuttled back as the craft was drowned in a sea of purple. It tried to swing left and right, but in the end, it was useless.

It fell down. Its tentacles started spraying out everywhere; then they went limp.

It was finished.

Cassie stopped firing the purple electricity. She rubbed her hands together, then walked over to me, holding out a slightly blackened palm. "You can thank me later."

I felt my cheeks blush and ignored Cassie's hand, pulling myself to my feet. "I had it."

"Oh yeah. Really looked like you had it. Anyway. Where were we?"

I took Cassie's hand and teleported her much easier this time. We ended up right outside Ellicia's home. It was strange, seeing it again after all this time. It felt like so long had passed, but at the same time, no time had passed at all.

I walked up her driveway, toward the main door.

Then I hopped through the walls and into her home.

Her kitchen was dark and empty. My footsteps echoed as I walked around. I moved from room to room, searching everywhere, and Cassie did the same.

But when I got back down to the kitchen, I knew what the outcome was from the way Cassie looked at me, and the way she shook her head.

Ellicia wasn't here.
She'd already gone.

[14]

It didn't take me long to find out what had happened to Ellicia.

I was back at the old, derelict office block that I'd been in before. Saint, Orion, and Daniel were still there, keeping a low profile. Only this time, Cassie was with me too, as was Damon.

"She got evacuated, mate," Damon kept saying, shaking his head, like it was the worst news in the world. "Her and Avi. Everyone in New York, taken out of here quicker than we could click our fingers."

I sank my teeth into my bottom lip. "I can't believe they'd just get evacuated so quickly."

"Maybe the government were prepared for something like this. Especially after the things that happened in the past."

Orion nodded. "Or perhaps they have a way of teleporting people to safe places, now. Using the abilities of ULTRAs to protect their own."

It was the first time he'd spoken for a while, but it made sense. It still seemed eerie, being back in his company. After all, this man was my biological father. And Daniel Peters was my biological brother.

It just didn't feel like any of it had sunk in yet.

"Anyway," Daniel said, sparking up some fire in his hand. "You should be happy, shouldn't you?"

I felt a flicker of shame. I cleared my throat, twitching either side. "Of course I'm happy."

"You don't seem like you're happy."

I couldn't act happy if I weren't. "You're right," I said. "I'm not happy. But not because Ellicia and Avi and Dad have been taken somewhere safe. Just... just everything. The fact that this is even happening. The fact I've only been back, what, a day, and already shit's going down. I've barely even had a chance to say hi to Ellicia again."

"Perhaps you were brought back for a reason," Saint said.

He was standing over by the window. The dark sky cast a peculiar shadow over him. Outside, there were occasional flashes and blasts as the enemy did their work, trying to purge this world of ULTRAkind—and not caring so much about who got caught in the crosshairs.

I frowned. "What do you mean I was brought back for a reason?"

Saint turned around and faced me. My toes still curled when he did. Another weird thing to get used to, suddenly being allied with the man who'd destroyed your life and attempted to destroy so many others. "I mean, perhaps it's no coincidence that you were out cold for eighteen months and just so happened to return a day before the greatest threat to our civilization since... well, me."

Daniel tutted. "Give me some credit, at least."

Saint ignored him. "I don't just mean you. I mean me. Your father. Your brother. Don't you think it's remarkable that we've all been brought back here—the four most powerful ULTRAs ever to have lived—right on the eve of destruction.

"Hey," Damon said, sparking up his electricity. "My powers might have something to say about that."

Again, Saint ignored him. He walked toward me and reached a point where he was opposite me, and Daniel was opposite Orion.

We stood together as men, the four of us, and I felt like I understood what he was saying.

"So now we face a choice," Saint said. "A choice we've pitched to you before."

"There is no choice," I said.

"What?"

"If there's a choice between letting the world crumble and... and fighting, then there's no other choice but to fight."

Saint sighed. He nodded. "Good. You've seen sense then, at last."

He turned around and walked away.

"We'll regroup in an hour. Take some time to refresh. Then, we'll discuss what we do next. How we proceed."

Everyone left the room except for Damon, Daniel, and Orion. I looked at Orion, and he looked back at me. There was something unspoken between us. It didn't even feel like we *had* to speak anymore to understand one another.

I headed into the bathroom area and looked in the mirror. I pulled off my Glacies mask, and I saw myself, and I felt so scared. This was me. Kyle Peters. Not Glacies. And Kyle Peters wasn't strong enough. He had never been strong enough.

So I put the mask on again, and I took a deep breath, accepting who I had to be, and the responsibilities I had.

I had to take a breather, and then I had to fight to save this world.

But it still felt, as I stared into the eyes of my alter-ego, like I could see Kyle Peters' shadow burning right through...

[15]

The following morning, I went looking for the members of the Resistance.

I say "morning," but of course, it wasn't as simple as that. There was a glimmer of daylight shining around the edges of the large spacecraft, but mostly it just created a deep amber glow, much like the nightmarish red I'd seen in my dreams.

The sky was filled with those smaller crafts, too. They flew around like drones, waving their metal tentacles in their wake. I could hear the hum from the craft, like it was connected to me almost. I'd asked the others if they could hear it too, but they insisted I was just imagining things.

I was certain I wasn't.

There was something linking me to this craft. Something I couldn't see yet.

We'd decided to each pursue a member of the Resistance. I was going after a guy called Rhynart. He had the ability to change the form of objects. I hadn't known him well, only that he'd been experiencing his abilities for years. The first time he'd realized he had his abilities was by accident. His father, who used to beat him, was taking a bath. When he'd got in there, after a round of whipping, Rhynart poured all his anger out and wished that his dad's bath filled with lava.

The awkward thing? It did.

Of course, the house was ruined, and Rhynart was soon moving out. He left home not long after, and was homeless from very young. He told me he tried to use his abilities on demand, but it wasn't as simple as that. They only surfaced in times of real need. I understood what he meant by that.

But he'd learned to hone his abilities. He'd become a strong member of the Resistance.

Now, I was hovering over the building in Phoenix, AZ, where I heard he'd transformed a cardboard box into a fully self-functioning home, preparing to convince him to join the fight. Saint, Cassie, Orion, Daniel, and Damon had each gone on a mission of their own. But this was mine.

Only I wasn't alone.

There was one of those crafts right outside his house.

I moved slowly in its direction, holding my breath. It didn't look like it'd seen me. If I could throw it through a wormhole quickly, then that would be ideal.

As I got closer, I saw the craft wasn't moving at all. It was totally still.

I felt a sense of unease carpet me, as I slowed my progression even more. That was weird. From what I'd seen of these things, they were very rarely still.

And that humming noise I usually heard when I got close to them. I wasn't getting that right now.

Still, I kept on moving. I stretched my arms out in front and focused my abilities, which seemed to be back to scratch after the scares I'd had over the last couple of days. I focused on the craft and went to blast it into oblivion.

Then I saw a movement behind it.

I went still.

There was someone in Rhynart's house, peeking through the window.

I lowered my arms, chuckled a little. "Jesus, Rhynart. At least make it move."

Then I dropped right beside the craft and walked past it, barely giving it any attention.

Because it wasn't a craft at all.

"Hey," Rhynart said. "I had a spare teddy bear and I saw what those things looked like. I at least had to *try* scaring you off."

Rhynart looked thinner than I remembered. His cheeks were gaunt, and he had long, curly ginger hair, with a little hair on his top lip. He was dressed in a checkered shirt, and scuttled around clumsily, like he always did. Not such a good thing for a guy who was prone to changing objects into other things to be, really, clumsy.

"So you were expecting me then?" I asked.

Rhynart scurried around his living room. It was open and spacious, with photographs of animals in their natural habitats hung up around the place. "I figured one of you would come for me."

"So you didn't think I was dead, then?"

Rhynart snorted. "You? Dead? Next joke, please."

I was pleasantly reassured by Rhynart's faith in me. He seemed like the first person who wasn't genuinely stunned that I was still living.

"Nah, I figured you were probably some part of a government lab somewhere. Or something along those lines, at least."

"I wish that were true," I said. "Really, it was a whole lot weirder."

"Tea?" Rhynart asked.

"No thanks."

"Right. Sure. Because you're not here to drink tea, are you?"

I knew I had to get to the point. "I'm guessing you've seen the—"

"Intergalactic spaceship that's threatening our entire kind with extinction? Yep. Just about clocked it."

"Then you'll know what we have to do."

Rhynart threw a few things into a rucksack and then zipped it up. "I know what I have to do. Run the hell away from this place, now you've led a trail to here."

He started to walk past me, but then I teleported myself right in front of him. I couldn't just let him leave.

Rhynart laughed a little, defeated, and lowered his head. "Right. Because you weren't gonna just let me leave without a fight, either."

"We need all the help we can get if we're going to fight this threat. You have to see that."

"Oh, I see it alright. I just don't want to be a part of it. Now if you'll let me leave my own home, please."

I was stunned by Rhynart's resistance. He pushed past me, and I couldn't help moving out of his way. "After all the fighting we've done together. After everything we've worked so hard for. You're just gonna walk away?"

"Yep," Rhynart said, reaching the door to his home. "Kyle—you don't mind if I call you Kyle, do you? Look. Sometimes, we fight. Other times, we have to know when it's time to stop fighting, or we'll end up killing ourselves."

"As opposed to this mothership butchering the lot of us himself, you mean?"

"I know you don't like the idea of seeming weak. But I can see it in your eyes. You want to run just as much as I do. Because you know this is a battle too far. Hey, we've had a good run. But we have to know when to decide between fighting to the death and fighting for our survival. And right now, the odds of a latter looks a whole lot better to me."

I couldn't say a word. I was just stunned. "After everything. You're just walking away."

"Too right. And you'll do the same, if you have any sense at all."

I wanted to stop Rhynart from walking. I wanted to convince him to come back. He could be an asset to the Resistance. He was a part of the fight.

But the worst thing?

I could see where he was coming from.

I looked down at the list of names of ULTRAs I'd already tried contacting. There were still some left. It wasn't game over yet. There were always going to be those who didn't want to get involved.

I was about to teleport away when I saw something.

One second, Rhynart was there.

But he wasn't alone.

There really was a craft opposite him.

My muscles tensed. My mind raced. I had to go over there. I had to help...

But it was already too late.

With the blink of an eye, Rhynart was gone.

And as he vanished, I could've sworn I heard him scream out my name.

[16]

I looked at the spot where Rhynart had vanished and I felt my stomach begin to turn.

The day had stretched on, and I hadn't been able to progress my search. I'd spent a little time out just trying to absorb everything that was happening, and everything that had happened.

In the end though, I just kept on coming back to that moment when I'd seen Rhynart there one second, reluctant to involve himself in the battle.

The next second, gone.

Screaming.

And I couldn't help wondering whether that was supposed to be me.

The desert air was hot and humid, a vast contrast to the rest of the country at this time of year. My throat was dry, and I was getting a headache. The smell of the scorched earth clung to the sides of my nostrils, making me think of *everything* that had burned since I'd become Glacies.

My home.

Mom, inside it.

I flinched when that thought entered my mind. I didn't like to think back to Mom too much. As much as painful memories charged and fueled my abilities, that one was just too painful.

I couldn't sit around here and mope for long, though. I knew I had to go back to Orion, Saint, Daniel, Cassie, and Damon. I had to see how they'd progressed in attracting old members of the Resistance to their side.

I teleported my way to the Galapagos. We'd agreed to use it as our base. We'd made sure we'd picked an island that didn't already look pretty inhabited by animals. Didn't want to disturb them.

When I got there, I saw conflict right away.

Someone was zooming through the sky, fighting off a craft. The craft was firing blasts out of its tentacle arms. They were shelling, hard.

I lifted my hands right away and sent a massive blast of ice in the craft's direction.

The craft turned to look at me. Then it flew toward me. Fast.

I pushed back with more ice, intensifying my assault. I could hear voices, but I didn't focus on them. Only on pushing back.

The craft kept on hurtling toward me.

I flinched back, losing my focus. I held my breath and waited for it to collide with me, which it no doubt was going to.

And then from the right, something smacked into the craft and shattered it into pieces.

I stood and looked at the fallen remains of the craft, smoke rising from it, and tried to process what I'd just witnessed.

"Thank me later. Or now. Preferably now. Kid."

It was Stone.

I grinned and walked up to him. "Good to see you here."

He rubbed his hands together and eased the stone away.

"Wish I could say the same about you. As it stands, we're in a pretty shitty all-round situation. So it's not that great, is it?"

"I guess it isn't."

"Is he moaning already?"

I looked over Stone's shoulder and I saw Vortex. Her hair was different. Looked like she'd dyed it blonde.

I still felt a quiver in my stomach whenever I saw Vortex. My cheeks flushed. "Hey. Good to see you again."

"You too, Glacies."

We stood together over the fallen craft, which was nothing more than wires and metalwork now. In the distance, I could see Saint, Orion, Daniel, Cassie and Damon, heading toward us.

"You all cool working for Saint all of a sudden?" Stone asked.

"We're not working *for* him."

Stone snorted. "Seems to be the man with the plan. You sure you trust him?"

I looked over at Saint. He was speaking with Daniel. He glanced up at me, then nodded.

"No," I said. "I never will. But what else do we have right now? Anyway. Is this everyone?"

"Not quite."

The voice made me flinch. I turned around and saw her.

Roadrunner was standing opposite me. She looked more muscular. Her hair was shorter. She had a scar across her face, which made me wonder where she'd been and what she'd seen. The time for questions would come.

I hugged Roadrunner, and so too did the others. Then we stood together in a circle, all nine of us, and looked down at the fallen craft.

"Did you not manage to find anyone, bro?" Daniel asked. There was a slight smile on his face.

I gritted my teeth. "Don't. Just don't."

His smile dropped, and he nodded. “Sorry. I sometimes forget my sense of humor is a little... alternative.”

After a few moments of reunion, it was Orion who walked to the middle of the circle.

“Now, I know this scenario isn’t something we ever anticipated. I know we’re being forced to swallow differences. But we aren’t going to defeat this threat if we stick around down here.”

“What’s that supposed to mean?” Stone asked.

Orion looked right at Stone. “I think you know what it means. We’re going to have to take the fight to the enemy.”

He looked up at the sky. We all looked up with him. Up there, I could see a small, circular blot, not much bigger than the moon. It was completely black.

“The mothership,” I mumbled.

“The enemy are hunting us down. They’re killing humans and animals in the crossfire, too. So as far as I see it, we don’t have a choice. We take the fight to their mothership, all nine of us. Are you in?”

There was a pause.

Then Saint stepped forward. “I’m in.”

Orion nodded. “Anyone else?”

Daniel stepped forward. Then Roadrunner. After that, Stone and Vortex, although Stone didn’t look best pleased about this arrangement.

Damon, Cassie and I still held back.

“We need you,” Saint said. “All three of you.”

I took a deep breath and clenched my fists.

Then together, in unison, the three of us stepped forward.

“Good,” Orion said. “Right.” He looked up. “Then it’s time we take the fight to them.”

[17]

Hielo looked down at the Earth below and a part of him felt a twinge of sadness to see all the conflict.

It was the middle of the day where the mothership was right now. They were positioned just outside the Earth's atmosphere, floating graciously above. Down below, the sun shimmered against the sea, making Hielo squint. It was beautiful to look at, though. So peaceful. So serene. Mother Nature really was a goddess.

He saw his soldiers hovering around in search of ULTRAs and his stomach knotted.

It wasn't that he felt guilty about wiping out ULTRAs. After all, it was what he had to do. He knew things the people on this planet didn't. He knew what happened if he let the ULTRAs live. He'd seen it before, so many times.

It might seem to the world right now that he was the villain, and that the ULTRAs would be their heroes again. But that was not how it worked. In time, history would remember him for the great act of kindness he'd gifted the planet.

History would remember him as a savior.

And if it didn't... well, being remembered didn't matter so much. At least he knew, deep down, that he was doing the right thing.

"Hielo?"

The voice behind him made him flinch. He turned around from his enormous window, which looked out over the planets. "What have you got for me?"

It was one of his soldiers, B837. Being spoken to by mechanically developed creatures wasn't strange to him anymore. He'd been surrounded by them for so many years that artificial intelligence was just the *way* now. If anything, it was the most advanced life form in the universe.

B837's cold, steely exterior glared at him. The tentacles were hanging by its side. "Someone who's been close, I believe. To the one you are searching for."

Hielo felt a tightness in his throat. He looked down, then quickly back up, to maintain an air of composure. "You're sure?"

"I can sense it on them. The presence you spoke about. Would you like me to bring him in here?"

Hielo felt both his tension and his anticipation rising. "No," he said. "I'll come to him."

"Absolutely, sir. I'll be right outside."

"That's okay, B837. You get back to work."

"Are you sure? I can—"

"Really. Thank you."

B837 didn't protest after that. He—yes, artificial intelligence was gendered now, too—just turned around and climbed out of the room.

Hielo looked back out of the window. He saw more of his soldiers leaving, falling to Earth. He saw explosions in South Africa. He wanted to go down there himself and intervene.

Now he had a chance. Someone who'd been close. Someone who could help him.

He walked out of his room and into the corridor. The walk down the corridor was long and drawn out. The walls were narrow, and the ceilings were low. It was made of metal, and that metal hadn't been painted. It was all very industrial, and not at all homely.

He didn't need it to be homely. Homeliness wasn't its purpose.

He stopped when he reached the room. He didn't have to ask which room to go to, where the captive was. He just knew already. He could feel their struggle. He could hear the tension in the air.

He took a deep breath and prepared himself for one of a number of people he could see.

And then he opened the door.

Rhynart was lying back against a metal frame.

He had bands wrapped around him, which flickered with electricity and made him gasp every time he tried to use a power. Hielo saw the bands changing form, just for a moment, and then the electricity kicked in and suppressed those abilities once again.

"There's no point fighting," Hielo said. "Those bands are crafted by a far, far stronger material than anything you're used to back home."

He walked over to the side of the table. Rhynart looked up at him, wide-eyed, with total fear.

"Hello, Rhynart."

"How do—how do you—"

"How I know who you are isn't the issue. I know you're a good soldier. And I know you're a good man. I also know you're an ULTRA, and that's a problem. Because I know what your kind are capable of."

He leaned in closer toward Rhynart.

"However, you can make this whole process a lot easier for

yourself. All you have to do is tell me the truth."

Rhynart gasped and struggled. "The truth about... about what?"

"About the last ULTRAs you came into contact with. About who they were."

Hielo saw the change in Rhynart's expression right away. He knew Rhynart knew what he was referred to, and who he was talking about.

"I don't... I didn't..."

Hielo lifted a hand and hovered it over Rhynart's head. "Don't do this to yourself. Don't make it any more difficult than it's going to be already. For both of us."

Rhynart lowered his gaze. Hielo could see him trying to figure out whether it was worth it, continuing lying, or to just open up and tell the truth.

Then he looked back up at Hielo, and Hielo knew he'd made his choice already. "I didn't see any ULTRAs. I haven't seen any ULTRAs for over six months."

Hielo sighed. "I'm sorry you gave that answer. For both of us. I really am."

Then he tightened his grip.

Rhynart's eyes shut right away. His face turned red, and then purple.

All the while, Rhynart searched his mind, scoured his memories, all to find out the face of the one he was looking for.

He knew, deep down, who it was. But he just needed to see for himself.

And he needed to be sure Rhynart was lying before he did what he did next.

For a while, as he saw flashes of Rhynart's last few months—alone, isolated, right in the desert—he started to actually believe Rhynart and wonder whether his soldiers had got it wrong all along.

But then he saw him.

One of his last memories. The fear of having that ULTRA turn up on his doorstep.

The ULTRA reaching out to him, just before Rhynart walked away.

Hielo sighed, and let loose his grip on Rhynart. He walked away from the side of Rhynart's bed, leaving him gasping.

"I told you there was no point lying," he said. "I've seen the truth now."

He looked up, then. Looked right up at the circular opening above. He could see a light glowing there. The more he focused on it, the closer that light got.

"The world is going to fall, you know. All because of ULTRAs like you."

"Please. Whatever it is you think I've done, I haven't. I—"

"I wish there were another way," Hielo said. And he meant that. He really did. "But this is the only way."

He put a hand on Rhynart's struggling chest.

"I'm sorry, old friend."

"Please. Please!"

Then Hielo put his full concentration into that light above.

He saw the light crawl down and slam into Rhynart's chest.

He heard Rhynart's screams and gasps as the power left his body.

And as the guilt ran through Hielo's body, he saw the image of that last ULTRA Rhynart had interacted with, and he knew for certain who he was after now.

He knew there could be no mistaking him.

The light stopped its assault, climbing back up into the shaft.

Rhynart let out a final gasp, then went still.

Hielo walked out of the room and back into his room, back over to the window.

He looked down at the Earth and he wondered where his target was, and what he was going to do to him.

Glacies.

[18]

I flew at the mothership, the eight remaining members of the Resistance by my side, and I hoped I was doing the right thing.

The further we got to the edge of the Earth's atmosphere, the darker things got.

It was all made even darker by the fact that we were getting nearer the mothership, which drooled pitch blackness.

The mothership was much like the smaller crafts that accompanied it. It was enormous, perfectly smooth, much like a rock of coal that had been dipped in varnish for a long, long time. There were tentacles shooting out of it, although these tentacles were as thick as islands. One punch by them would be enough to cause a tidal wave of epic proportions.

Or shatter a few ULTRA bones.

I shuddered at the thought. I couldn't let that happen. None of us could.

We all flew together, covered by my invisibility, which I had cast over everyone. We didn't want to rush into teleportation because with teleportation came risks. I'd discovered that first hand in the battle with Catalyst when I'd gone teleporting head-first into a volcano and found myself in a trap.

Sure, the initial plan was teleportation. But like all the best plans, they developed over time.

"So what's the plan?" Stone shouted.

"We told you the plan," Daniel said. "We hit the mothership hard. Test its defenses. Then we know what we're up against."

"Oh. Damn," Stone said. "*That* was the plan? I thought we were just throwing mud at a wall and seeing what stuck."

"It's the best idea we've got," Roadrunner said. "Unless you can think of anything better."

"What do you think, Glacies?" Vortex muttered. "You still fancy yourself as a genius?"

I hadn't said much, to be fair. I thought the plan was solid enough. Testing the defenses of the mothership was wise. But I was trepidatious, too. I couldn't stop feeling like I was Kyle, and not Glacies. And sure, I'd faced up to the fact I had to fight, now. But there were still so many issues and problems with this whole situation that I didn't want to face.

Issues and problems that I didn't think I had the strength to handle.

"Shit. Crafts ahead."

I saw them right as Roadrunner spoke.

Three of those metal crafts, all flying toward us.

That sense of foreboding kicked in right away as I slowed to a halt. In turn, everyone slowed, as I was using my powers to make the whole lot of us go quicker.

"Um, did you mean to slow, Glacies?"

"I'm going to jump over them," I said.

"What?"

"Just trust me. Okay?"

The crafts got closer. They seemed to be picking up pace as they approached. I had to time this right.

"I don't trust you," Daniel said. "That's part of the problem."

I ignored Daniel's quip and closed my eyes.

Then I jumped us all through a small wormhole, right to the other side of the crafts.

I opened my eyes. I was cautious about the effects of my wormhole jumping, which seemed to have been hit and miss lately.

The crafts were right opposite us.

My stomach sank.

"Shit," Stone said. "This is why we don't goddamned trust you!"

A craft was just inches from my face.

I pulled back my fist and slammed it into it, charging it up with all my powers and wrapping my knuckles in the hardest ice I could forge.

The craft slipped out of the way, then slammed me between the legs with its long tentacle.

The pain was instant and insufferable. I winced and gripped my stomach. I tried to charge up my energy again.

Then another of the tentacles grabbed me by the throat and lifted me into the air.

My heart pounded. I tried to shuffle my way free again. I couldn't do this. I was trapped. I was trapped and I wasn't Glacies, I was Kyle. I was Kyle and I was weak and I...

No.

I wasn't Kyle.

I *was* Glacies.

I grabbed the tentacle and started to freeze it. I bit down my lip and pushed even harder. All around me, I was aware of the rest of the Resistance fighting off the crafts. Saint, though, was alone. He wasn't helping me or anyone. He was just observing, like he was waiting for something bad to happen.

The tentacle slipped free of my hand.

No!

I reached for it with my telekinesis and yanked it back.

Then I poured a blast of ice at it.

I saw the tentacle recoil. I stretched it out, further freezing the section of the tentacle I'd stretched.

I kept on twisting it, kept on turning it, kept on believing.

I saw another tentacle swing around and try to grab it.

I lifted my hand, stopped it right in the air.

I felt blood dripping down my face and tasted it on my lips. I twisted around, facing the craft head on, heart pounding, muscles tensed.

"Go to hell," I said.

I cracked my hands to either side.

The tentacles pulled free of the craft.

A sharp noise, like a cry, emitted from it.

Then the smooth, black body of the craft fell out of the sky and went crashing down to the Earth below.

"Good job," Damon muttered, appearing beside me. "Only two more to go."

My body recoiled. I turned around ready to fight off some more, even though I knew I didn't have the energy.

"Just kidding," Damon said, patting my back. "We sorted the others far quicker than you sorted that. What's got into you, mate?"

I looked around at the eight other Resistance members, all of them floating, all still intact.

Then I looked down and saw the bodies of the crafts spiraling down to the ground below.

"Kyle?" Cassie said. "You okay?"

I didn't know what she was talking about at first. Then I tasted the blood again, which had congealed around my lips.

When I tasted it, I started to feel faint.

"Shit," Cassie said. "I think he needs some help..."

She said something else. I wasn't sure what.

Because even though my body was here, my mind was elsewhere.

I looked up at the mothership.

All I could describe this feeling as was déjà vu. Serious déjà vu.

I'd been here before. I'd seen this before.

This wasn't just déjà vu.

This was a flashback...

I saw a tentacle reaching out of the side of the big mothership, then. The others were all around me, all looking at me, so they couldn't see it.

I tried to warn them. Tried to point at it. But I was just too weak.

"What's he trying to say?" Stone said. "What's he..."

Then he turned around, before anyone else.

"Oh. Oh sh—"

The tentacle slammed into all of us.

I felt a heavy crack to my head.

Then, darkness.

[19]

I saw darkness, and then I saw light.

I was in a room. I was standing over someone. Someone I recognized. They were strapped to a table, strange looking bands wrapped over their body.

It took me a few moments to realize that the someone I was looking at was Rhynart.

I saw that he was struggling, and that made me feel uneasy. This whole scenario felt dreamlike, but I was aware that I was unconscious, so it wasn't any normal dream.

I hovered over the top of the table as Rhynart struggled and fought.

And then before I could help him, I found myself turning upwards, looking up at the opening above.

There was a light in that opening. It beamed down toward me. Although it was perfectly bright—so bright I could barely look at it—it had a form similar to the darkness that I'd seen growing from this mothership when I'd first seen it.

It was pure light. And it was strong.

I saw the light coming down that hatch and my body tensed. I heard Rhynart's screams getting louder, and I knew I had to go. I wasn't supposed to be here. This wasn't for me to witness.

And still, I couldn't help watching.

I saw the light reach out its formless hand and pull Rhynart's body up against those bands.

I saw him trying to resist, electricity stretching across his chest, as something was pulled from his body. Something else light.

I saw it get yanked away from him.

And then the light disappeared up into the belly of the mothership, and I felt total power, and then—

"They're harvesting our powers."

Suddenly, I saw Cassie looking over me. Behind her, the rest of the Resistance. I wasn't in that mothership or in that dream anymore. I was back in reality.

"Damn," Stone said, stepping to my side. "The kid's actually awake."

"The mothership," I said, unable to control my words. "It's harvesting our abilities. That's why... that's why it's hunting us."

I saw the confused glances and the furrowed eyebrows. Behind these people, I could see that I was on an island. Back on one of the Galapagos, clearly.

"What did you just say?" Cassie asked.

I regained my breath and composure. My heart was still pounding rapidly. "I just... I don't know."

"You said something about them harvesting our abilities. Is that a theory?"

"No. I just know."

"How do you know?"

I didn't know what to say. I definitely couldn't say "I'd dreamt it." "I don't know how I know. I just... I just do."

More looks of confusion and amazement.

Daniel snorted. "No offense, brother, but you were the first to fall unconscious when we got knocked out of the sky. You've been lying down there pretty much ever since. And we've kept a close eye on you, don't you worry."

I knew how ridiculous I sounded, as I struggled to my feet. My head ached, and I felt tired and fatigued.

"Whatever Kyle claims he does or doesn't know," Stone said, "we've seen how strong their defenses are."

"So what?" Orion said. "We just give up?"

"I'm just saying. We were lucky not to become alien jello last time round. We'd be very, very goddamned lucky if we escaped that fate again."

I could hear the trepidation and I knew our assault on the mothership, brief as it had been, had already caused tensions amidst the group.

"I don't think we should give up, necessarily," Stone said. "Just... just go back to the drawing board. Completely."

I heard the false optimism in his voice, and I could see that it hadn't exactly inspired the rest of the group.

"So does anyone have any other ideas?"

There was silence. I saw them looking at me, but I didn't know what to say either. What *did* we do?

"Maybe I can offer a suggestion."

I looked over at Saint. As did everyone else.

He didn't exactly look confident about what he had in mind.

"I'm sure you're full of suggestions," Roadrunner said.

"It's not a conventional idea. But just hear me out. When... when, you know, I tried to take this planet."

"Saint Attack v1 or Saint Attack v2?" Damon asked.

"The second time. I was aided by an army. Do you remember?"

"The ULTRAbots," I said. "How could we forget?"

"What do the ULTRAbots have to do with anything,

anyway?" Stone asked. "They're all gone. Finished. We beat 'em."

Saint looked toward the ground.

"Aren't they?"

He looked back up. "Not exactly."

"What? But they—"

"There were some I kept just in case."

"Like how governments held on to a bit of smallpox," Damon said. "Just in case?"

"They were unactivated. They were untrained. And if they were untrained, that means..."

"They can still be trained," I said.

Saint nodded. "They can be trained to target an enemy. A very specific enemy."

I saw the path opening up in front of us. I saw the realization spreading across the group.

All of us saw what we had to do now.

"So who's ready to go awaken some ULTRAbots?"

[20]

If you'd told me just an hour ago that I'd soon be hunting down a hidden ULTRAbot lab that Saint had kept secret from the world, I would've told you that you were mad.

But such was the craziness of things right now, all of a sudden it felt kind of... well. Normal.

The first light of the sun was peeking over the Indonesian horizon. The Resistance—all nine of us—hovered above a stretch of sea that Saint had identified as where we needed to go. The sun was burning hot on the back of my neck, which not even a little of my ice could cool down. The silence of the place was intense and made me feel even more pressure than I'd felt already. I could smell the salt from the sea and taste it on my lips, even though I hadn't submerged in that water.

Yet.

"So you expect us to just dunk ourselves down there, swim to the bottom of the sea and hope for the best?"

Stone's bafflement and skepticism captured the mood of everyone. Vortex scratched the back of her neck, looking uncertain. Damon glanced from Cassie to me and back again. Even Daniel didn't seem all that keen on this plan.

Saint drifted down toward the water, hovering just above it. "This was never going to be easy. If you thought it was going to be easy, then you really should have stayed at home."

"My issue's not so much with it looking *easy* or not," Roadrunner said. "Rather, I just don't really want to drown myself anytime soon."

Saint tilted his head to one side. "If we get to the bottom of the ocean soon enough, then we won't drown at all." He looked to me then. "Glacies?"

I felt my skin crawl as the eyes of the others focused on me, waiting for me to make a decision. I couldn't lie—I had the same concerns as everyone else. After all, nigh-on drowning myself because Saint said he had a load of old unactivated ULTRAbots hidden under the sea, just waiting for someone to send them to fight... it seemed like a stretch.

But then, I'd seen the enemy we were up against. I'd seen how eager they were to wipe out all of ULTRAkind. And I didn't think they were discriminating between Saint and everyone else.

"It's the only option we have," I said.

Stone shook his head. "Technically, it's not."

"Got any better ideas?"

"We could always go home and drown ourselves in the bath. Least that way I won't get salt in my eyes."

I shook my head then flew down to Saint's side.

Of course I was reluctant.

Of course I had reservations.

But it seemed like the only half-decent plan we had right now in the defense against the enemy.

I waited down there a few seconds, looking up at everyone else and watching them.

"I always knew you were intelligent," Saint said. "I always knew there was more to you than meets the eye."

"Don't think this makes us allies or anything like that."

Saint chuckled a little. "Oh, don't you worry. I wouldn't think a thing like that."

Gradually, one by one, the rest of the Resistance drifted down to our side. Before I knew it, we were all right there, just above the water, staring at our rippled reflections.

"The plan is, we shoot directly down. Roadrunner is the fastest here, so we'd do much worse than holding on to her as she leads the way. That okay?"

Roadrunner puffed out her lips. "Doesn't really seem like I've got much of a choice."

Saint nodded, clearly taking that as a resounding "yes." "Okay," he said. "Then we link our arms and we make the move. Hold your breath. Because this facility is quite a way down."

I took Cassie's hand on one side and Saint's on the other.

Saint tightened his grip.

"If you even think about doing anything," I said.

"Oh, I wouldn't do a thing. We're friends now. Right?"

I felt sick even thinking of being friends with Saint. I tightened my grip on his hand though, just to assert my authority above anything. "Don't push your luck."

Saint chuckled. "On my count. Three, two—"

What happened next happened so quickly.

There was a blast. A large splash of water flew up and hit me right in the face. At first, I was just confused. I didn't know what it was, and my instinctive gut reaction made me let go of Saint's hand because I was convinced he must've double-crossed us in some way.

When I spun around, I saw three of those metal, tentacular craft surging in our direction.

My stomach sank as the one in the middle opened a mouth I didn't even realize it had and fired out rapid blasts of perfectly round, green energy.

The first of the energy balls slammed past us. It threw us all to the sides. *Shit.* Whatever that energy was, it was strong. Stronger than anything we were used to.

I saw more of the energy balls hurtling toward the Resistance and I knew, as cautious as I was, that I couldn't just stand by and watch.

I had to fight back.

An energy ball fired out of the craft's mouth, making a beeline for Vortex.

I lifted my hands and fired a blast of ice and telekinesis at it.

But the ice melted before it could reach it.

And the energy ball was just so, so heavy.

The ball flew past Vortex—just past her—and fell into the sea. It kicked up a massive wave, as did more of those energy balls as they fell.

"They're too tough," Daniel shouted. "I don't think we can—"

I saw an energy ball moving near to him.

Then I saw it slam against him.

My body went numb. All the sounds in my ears disappeared.

I watched the energy ball slam into Daniel, again and again, and again.

My brother.

I don't know what drove me to do what I did next. I don't even know where I found the strength.

But I did.

I found myself crying out as I reached into what felt like Daniel's body.

As I cracked my way through inside it with my mind, trying to repair the damage and reverse what'd happened.

I saw the sky turning gray. I saw lightning all around.

I heard a voice in my mind—a voice like the one that'd

spoken to my from the mothership—and I felt a tingling sensation all through my body like I'd never heard before.

I screamed out even louder as I tried and tried to reverse what'd happened to Daniel—as I tried to save him.

Then, something strange happened.

I saw the green energy ball move back out of Daniel's chest.

I saw his body lifting upwards like things were... *reversing*.

I let my grip loose then, baffled and staggered by what I'd just seen.

The energy ball fired at Daniel again.

This time, I lifted my hands and I stopped it.

I held that energy ball with my mind. My entire body was tensed. My nose was bleeding again.

But I was moving the energy ball, and everyone else around me was... still. Totally still.

I pulled that energy ball back with all the strength I had. It was the heaviest thing I'd ever carried. Even heavier than that damned Kilimanjaro debris I'd saved myself from back in one of my old scraps with Nycto.

I moved it up to the sides of the crafts, all of them in a row.

I spun the metal ball around. Even though it wasn't in my hands, I felt the skin being sliced away by them, like I was pushing them up against a hot sander.

I put it in place.

I let out a cry.

And then I let go.

I blinked, and I missed it.

But when I opened my eyes, I knew what'd happened right away.

There was a hole in each of the crafts.

All of them were hovering there one moment.

The next, they were falling into the sea.

There was silence for a while. Total quietness as we figured out what'd just happened.

Then, Stone lifted his head and looked right at me. "What the hell just happened?"

I wished I could've answered.

We quickly linked arms again, then fired our way down into the sea. I didn't have the same trepidation as we headed downward this time. After what I'd just done—saving Daniel's life even *after* the damage had been done—I had to admit I was on a bit of a high.

But it was tinged with sadness, too.

If I had those abilities all along, then who else could I have saved?

Mom?

My thoughts were soon interrupted when we slammed against solid ground and landed inside some kind of underwater building.

"Damn," Damon said, rubbing at his eyes. "Why couldn't they just build it in, like, a mountain or something?"

Saint ignored him. "Quick. We should get them awake as soon as we can. I don't want to risk running into any more of those crafts."

As I started to walk, I felt Daniel grab my arm. I turned and faced him for a second.

"Whatever happened back there," he said, his voice low. "Whatever happened... I know you helped. So thank you. Really."

Then he walked off after Saint.

Wow. Even my psycho brother was thanking me.

We all followed Saint through a number of doors, down a maze of corridors.

"This place is *big*," Roadrunner said.

"It needed to be," Saint said, hopping through security doors and making turns that just seemed to be instinctive to him even though these corridors were all the same. "There couldn't be any risk of anyone else finding these things. Anyone but..."

He stopped.

I soon saw why.

The room ahead was enormous. It was hard to believe there was room enough in the ocean for it.

But there was no mistaking what this room contained.

There were stacks and stacks of glass capsules.

Inside each of those capsules, engulfed in water, there were ULTRAbots.

I felt nervous. My skin crept as I remembered the battles we'd had with those ULTRAbots, which Saint had been using as his armies all along back when he disguised himself as Mr. Parsons.

Saint smiled. "Come on. We have to awaken and program them. We can't delay much longer."

We all reluctantly followed Saint over to a huge screen, which I guessed was the activation hub.

"How long will this take?" Roadrunner asked.

"Any time between five minutes and five days."

"Five *days?*" Damon scoffed. "We'll be lucky if the world's still here by then."

"Then we just have to hope for the best," Saint said.

He lifted a hand and went to place it on the screen.

I felt fear and tension fill my body.

His hand came within inches of the screen.

Then I heard a thump.

I didn't know where it came from at first. I didn't know where it was.

But then I heard another.

And another.

My heart started pounding. My palms went sweaty.

I looked up, slowly, not wanting to see what I knew all along I was going to see.

"Shit," Stone said. "They found us. They goddamned found us."

Stone was right.

On the glass ceiling of this room, there were three of those crafts.

And their tentacles were slicing away at the glass, trying to break inside.

[21]

"So, did you account for evil metal octopuses attacking this place when you dragged us a zillion feet under the sea?"

I heard Stone's disdain toward Saint's rapidly failing plan, and I couldn't help agreeing with him. The crafts were slamming down into the glass ceiling on top of the hidden ULTRAbot facility. Soon, they would break through, and not only would the whole weight of the ocean fall down on us, but so too would a shitload of those enemy crafts.

I heard the bangs of the crafts against the glass. I could hear their metal claws slicing at the glass, and the sound of it went right through me. I wiped the salt away from my drying lips and I looked at Saint.

He stared up at the falling crafts, transfixed, like this wasn't a part of his plan at all.

"Saint," Orion said, walking to Saint's side. "We're going to have to do something. We can't just stand here. We have to act."

I could see the disappointment in Saint's eyes. And I never thought I'd say it, but I felt that disappointment too. This was supposed to be the moment where we made our grand fight back, taking the ULTRAbots out of this facility and training them to attack the enemy.

Instead, it didn't look like we had much time at all, and the ULTRAbots still hadn't been activated.

Another thump against the ceiling, which made me flinch. I looked and saw more of those tentacles slicing away. I swore I could hear water dripping to the floor below. We had barely any time left.

"There's two options," Saint said.

"Then share them quick," I said.

"First option is we proceed with the plan."

Cassie shook her head. "But you said that could take—"

"Up to five days," Saint said. "Right. Which is what takes us to plan B."

His voice broke uncharacteristically when he said "plan B."

"What's plan B?" I asked.

Saint paused for a few seconds.

Another craft hit the glass ceiling.

Time was running out.

"Saint," I shouted. "What's the plan B?"

"The plan B is to overdrive the activation and immediately wake the ULTRAbots. But they will be wild, and they will be untrained. And they will attempt to destroy everything in their path. Including people. And including us."

My stomach knotted. "So it's a choice between probably dying here and... probably dying here."

"I don't like either plan," Saint said. "But I think... I think plan B's all we've got."

I gritted my teeth together. "You knew this was going to happen all along, didn't you?"

Saint frowned. "What—"

"You brought us down here. You planned for us all to die

here and for your ULTRAbots to destroy everything else on this planet. All for your own gain. Didn't you?"

I saw, at the bottom of his mask, a smile creep across Saint's face then. "Kyle. Dear Kyle. I might be power-crazy, but I certainly am not suicidal."

I still didn't believe him.

I didn't have to.

The glass cracked, and water started to flood down.

I looked up and saw that water falling in slow motion. I lifted my hands and tried to return to the state of mind I'd been in before when I'd managed to reverse time somehow.

But I couldn't.

The water and the crafts were falling toward us.

"What should I do?" Saint shouted.

I looked up at the water, then back at him.

"Glacies. Make the call. What should I do?"

I swallowed a lump in my throat and held my breath. "Activate the overdrive."

Saint put his hands on the monitor. He tapped at it a few times as the water hurtled closer.

Then I saw him look up at the ULTRAbots and whisper, "God help us all."

The ULTRAbots were still. Totally still.

And then, their eyes opened, and I knew it had almost begun.

[22]

I held my breath as the ULTRAbots opened their eyes and hurtled out of their containers.

Darkness filled the ULTRAbot facility as both the enemy crafts and the mass of water fell toward us. It was impossible to tell what the conditions outside were like. And it didn't really matter anymore, either.

This was a world in itself. And it was a world we needed to escape. Fast.

The Resistance all stood in a line as the water and the crafts fell out. To the right, the ULTRAbots clawed their way out of their capsules. Some of them immediately shot in the direction of the crafts and engaged in conflict. Some of them were batted away in an instant. Others clung on, and seemed to be making progress.

Then a few of the ULTRAbots turned their attention to me and the rest of the Resistance and we knew our time here was over.

"Quick," I said. I reached out a hand to Cassie; then the others grabbed her hand. "We need to get out of here while we can."

"What about the ULTRAbots?" Damon asked.

I looked at them as they flew at the crafts. It was impossible at this stage to say who was winning, and who had the upper ground. But we couldn't stick around to find out who won. "We'll see what happens. But we have to—"

I felt a burning sensation slam into my chest.

A large, black cloud was right in front of me, screaming at me.

I felt total fear inside. I tumbled back, shaking. I tried to climb back to my feet and stand my ground, to push back.

Then the cloud wrapped around my neck and I heard the voice of the leader of the mothership speak again.

"Do not resist," it said. "You're only resisting the inevitable..."

I tensed my fists around that black cloud, unable to give up.

"Kyle!"

Cassie's voice snapped me from my trance. I gasped for air, looking around, disoriented.

The black cloud was nowhere to be seen.

"We need to get out of here!" she screamed.

The water was just meters above her head.

"We need to get..."

Then, it happened again.

I saw the water slamming into Cassie, Orion, Daniel.

I heard their necks breaking as their heads jolted forward.

I felt that strength inside—an unfamiliar, alien strength that was more raw and more powerful than anything I was used to.

And then I pushed back, and their necks moved back into place.

The water lifted upwards.

Only this time, I didn't give up.

I took deep breaths. I pushed that water back up, feeling everything reverse as I did so. My heart raced. I was reversing time. That's what this was. All along and I didn't know I had the ability to actually reverse time.

In the space of a second, drifting for a moment, I wondered just how far I could reverse time. Whether I could go right back and change things that'd gone wrong; fix the things I'd broken.

And then I lost my grip and the water started to fall again.

I grabbed Cassie's hand, and Orion's hand, and then they held on to the hands of the others.

"Quick!" Damon shouted.

I closed my eyes.

Held my breath.

And then I teleported the lot of us away from here, right as the water thumped against the floor.

When I opened my eyes, I was hovering in the sky right above the underwater ULTRAbot facility. I could tell from the movement and activity of the sea that this was the place.

Not just that, but the floating bodies of both ULTRAbots and crafts drifting to the surface.

"The ULTRAbot plan," Roadrunner said. "Do you... do you think it worked?"

I looked at Saint, feeling a strange, uneasy sense of disappointment on his behalf. He'd had an idea. A good idea. He'd tried to make it work. The idea had failed.

I knew how that felt. And I knew how vulnerable and planless that left us all.

"We'd better get away from here," Vortex said. "Before..."

I heard the screeching of movement above me and my stomach sank.

"Ah, hell," Stone said. "Looks like we're too late."

A whole crowd of the crafts was blasting toward us.

I saw them open up their metallic mouths. I saw the green balls of energy charging up and the crafts getting ready to fire. I saw it all unfolding.

But this time, I didn't feel attached in any way.

This time, I didn't let my thoughts get in my way.

I just lifted my hand and tensed my grip.

The first of the crafts crumpled up right away. The second one followed not long after, as I moved from one to the next, slowly, methodically, calmly.

Stone looked on in awe. "Is... Is he doing this?"

I kept on moving, not being distracted by the voices of my peers. I felt my strength and my abilities growing. In a way, they felt stronger than they ever had.

As long as I forgot I was just Kyle Peters underneath.

As long as I stayed under the guise of Glacies.

I saw the final craft send out a burst of green energy balls, like it knew it was on its last legs and didn't have long to live.

I saw them blasting down toward us, fast, and I wasn't sure I was going to be able to stop them all with my mind.

So I moved in front of them, opened up a wormhole, and then another wormhole right behind the craft, like it took up no energy at all when usually it crippled me.

The green energy balls fell through the wormhole.

They appeared through the other one.

The craft tried to move out of the way, quickly becoming aware of what was happening.

But not quickly enough.

The energy balls blasted the craft again and again, sending shards of metal off it, dismembering its tentacles and rendering it a useless piece of scrap.

I lowered my arms.

"Holy shit," Damon said, laughing and clapping. "That was amazing. That was... Kyle?"

My eyes closed.

I felt myself falling down to the sea.

But I was falling somewhere else, too.

I was falling into darkness...

Only when I landed, I wasn't alone.

There was someone opposite me. Someone dressed all in black. They were about my height.

And even though they hadn't spoken, I knew right away that they were the speaker from the mothership.

I was in a totally pitch black room. It was massive, making even the enormous ULTRAbot facility seem small in comparison.

The man walked in my direction, feet hitting the ground with a heaviness that suggested they were stronger than their slender frame. That they had secrets in their body.

He stopped right in front of me and looked into my eyes.

For a split second—just a split second—I saw something.

Something that filled me with fear.

Something that filled me with total dread.

I tried to shoot myself away from here.

But I couldn't. The man had his hand raised. He was tightening his grip around my neck using telekinesis. I was trapped.

As the air drifted from my body and I struggled for breath, I saw that terrifying thing again. It was something so terrifying that whenever I saw it, I forgot what it was right away, only to be reminded again almost instantly. It was as if my brain was trying to hide the truth from me because the truth was just too terrifying to realize.

I tried to lift my arms, but they were stuck. I tried to kick out my legs, but no use. I tried to activate my powers—any of my powers—but they were being sucked out of my body faster than I could do anything about them.

So in the end, all I could do was hover there in the grip of this man and wait...

"Give up, Kyle," he whispered. "It's time, now. Time to give up. I'm sorry I have to..."

I heard a glimmer of sensitivity in his voice, and for a moment, I felt calm and at ease like this was how things were meant to happen all along.

And then the grip tightened around my neck again, and the blackness suffocated me.

[23]

I opened my eyes and gasped for breath.

Water splashed against my face. I lunged forward, wheezing, trying to get a grip on myself.

"Whoa. Watch it, Kyle. Watch it. You're okay. We've got you."

I blinked. It was really bright. I was lying back on some kind of rock. I was still outside. The sea was crashing up against the shore. The sun was bright. All around me, the rest of the Resistance stood.

Daniel was by my side.

He had a hand on my shoulder, which he pulled away the second I looked at it.

"What..." I started. "What happened?" My lips were dry, and I could taste vomit at the back of my throat.

"You were in the air and you did some amazing shit to take down all the crafts, and then just... just... you had some weird kind of seizure. Like you were short-circuiting or something."

I still felt sick, so I leaned forward and put my head in my hands. I took a few deep breaths, as hard as they were to maintain, right in through my nose and out through my mouth. "How long was I out?"

"An hour. Two hours. We thought about taking you to some hospital or something, but we decided not to. At least you're here now, hey?"

I looked around at the rest of the Resistance. Damon. Cassie. Roadrunner. Stone. Vortex. Orion. Saint. All of them were silent. All of them were looking at me with concern. I could sense they didn't have the same faith in me that they used to have. I didn't want to admit it aloud, but I felt the same way about myself as they did.

"I feel it, too," Daniel said.

I frowned. "Feel what?"

His breathing was shallow and shaky. "There's pressure in the air. Pressure that I'm not used to. It feels like something just isn't... right. Like the whole world's on the verge of splitting. And still, I can't explain it. Like it's—"

"Happened before," I said.

Daniel closed his mouth and nodded. He couldn't maintain eye contact with me for something long. "There was something else, too. When we were back at that base. Before you had your seizure. The others don't see it, but I did. Just for a second."

Stone groaned. "He's not on about his double-vision again, is he?"

"What're you talking about?" I asked.

"Nycto thinks he saw two of you. Or some crap like that."

I looked back at Daniel. "What's this about."

Daniel glanced down at the ground. "When you were having your seizure. For a split second... just a split second, I swore I saw you. Like, a silhouette of yourself. Only you were fighting yourself. And then I blinked and the shadow was gone."

I felt the nausea intensifying, and I leaned over, knowing I was going to be sick.

"Regardless," Orion said, walking over to me and Daniel. "We've found a weakness in the crafts."

"Water," Saint said.

I narrowed my eyes. "Water? Really?"

Roadrunner nodded. "We ran into some trouble on our way out. When you were in the land of nod. Seems like water dulls their reactions, somehow. Makes them weaker, even if just for a few seconds. If water makes the crafts weaker, then we're thinking a shitload of water might be enough to make the mothership's defense weaker."

A silence stretched on for a few seconds after that.

"I know it's a long shot," Roadrunner said. "And damn. Times like this make me wish Aqua was still with us."

"Amen to that," Stone said.

"But right now, all we've got is the ability to try. Are you ready to help us, Glacies?"

I wasn't. I mean, was anybody?

But of course, I had to be ready.

I had to be as ready as I could be.

I stumbled to my shaky legs and I walked over to Roadrunner.

"I'm ready," I said.

She smiled. "Good. Then let's go get some H_2O. I think I know just the place."

[24]

"No chance. Absolutely out of the question."

"Come on. You have to see—"

"I've seen the level of destruction you're capable of. If you think we're just going to hand over our water cannons, then you must be either seriously dumb or seriously deluded."

"Aren't they the same thing?"

"It doesn't matter. The answer's the same. I'll not give you control of the water cannons. Not in a million years. And by God, you have a nerve just teleporting your way in here. Do you know how many White House security barriers you tripped on your way in?"

I stood opposite the President of the United States of America inside the Oval Office. Honestly, the Oval Office was just as spectacular in reality as it was when you saw it on the television and in the movies. Even more so, in fact, because all those television and movie versions were just that— *versions* of reality. This was the real thing, and it was staggering.

I'd come here to bargain with the president about the use of the high-intensity water cannons in the government's arsenal.

I'd been uncertain about the act, especially since the president not only thought I was dead, but mostly hated me. But really, there was more to this meeting than it seemed.

"The enemy threat," I said. "The mothership. I don't think you understand quite how dangerous it could be to all of us."

"Oh, I understand alright. What I understand is that this mothership is keen to wipe ULTRAs from the planet. And from what I understand, it didn't say a thing about its plans for humanity."

"So you'll just let us fall?"

He finished peeling an orange, then pulled away a segment and popped it into his mouth. "It's evolution. Survival of the fittest. Looks like you really weren't meant to outlive humanity after all, hmm?"

I held my tongue. The latest president—President West—had stepped in when the last president got killed in the battle with Adam. He was much more hardline toward ULTRAs. He didn't trust them because they threatened his power, and anything that threatened his power was evil in his eyes.

"And what about the people who are falling, too? The humans that are dying in the crossfire? Are they just natural casualties, too?"

The president wiped the orange from his fingers onto his white shirt, sighing when he realized the mistake he'd made, and he stood up and walked around the table. "Look, Glacies. Kyle. Whatever. I appreciate you coming here. I appreciate you actually *asking* my permission. Really, that's a neat touch. But I will *not* simply hand over our water cannons to someone like you."

"Someone like me?"

The president looked at me with a glance of disgust. "You know what I mean. Your kind." He smiled, patronizingly, like that'd just make everything better all of a sudden.

I kept my nerve and took deep breaths in and out. "See, I

thought you'd say that. But I wanted to ask nicely anyway. Because I really thought we could make some headway and come to an agreement."

The president narrowed his eyes. "What are you saying?"

I lifted my finger and pointed behind him. "I'm saying to remember where the real power is, Mr. President."

He turned around slowly, and he saw what I saw.

Stone was moving upward, floating outside the window of the White House.

Stacked atop his solid rock arms, there was a mass of water cannons.

"Holy..."

"Goodbye, Mr. President," I said. "I'll be sure to return the cannons in one piece."

"Don't you disapp—"

But I'd already teleported myself outside.

I appeared beside Stone. "You okay with that?"

"Kid, I've lifted a nuclear facility. I can cope with a bit of—"

Stone stumbled to one side.

One of the water cannons fell off the pile on top and came zooming down toward me.

I lifted my hands instinctively and fired a load of ice at it, tying it to the others, then I bound the rest of them with ice so they'd stay relatively together.

"Cheers, kid," Stone said. "But I had it. Really."

"That's them!" a voice shouted. "Stop them!"

I looked down at the White House grounds.

There was a team of soldiers right outside. All of them were holding guns.

And then the next second, they were firing in our direction.

I saw the bullets piercing through the air, racing after us. Part of me wanted to see if I could use that weird, time-reversing ability again.

But now wasn't the time or the place. I knew that well.

So I grabbed Stone's arm and I teleported us away from here.

We didn't get far.

I felt that punch-like sensation in my stomach and tasted blood from my nose on my lips. We were on the road now, just outside the White House grounds.

"Might wanna hurry, Kyle!" Stone shouted.

I gathered my composure, then went to teleport us again.

This time, a splitting headache kicked in before I could even get anywhere.

I saw the guards getting closer to us. They were firing anti-ULTRA ammo at us, which had the power to lower our abilities for a few seconds. Get hit with a few of them, and you'd be down for the count.

"What do we do, nerd?" Stone asked.

I looked up. It was the only idea I had. "We fly."

I crouched down and then bounced up, Stone by my side.

Those anti-ULTRA bullets flew past us. Some of them singed my costume as I moved, distorting my flight for a couple of seconds.

"Okay," Stone said. "This is good. This is progress. Now which direction?"

I was distracted, though.

I could see something coming my way.

"Is that a..." Stone started.

He'd seen it too.

It was a missile.

I lifted my hand to push it back.

The missile kept flying at us.

I pulled my attention fully away from Stone and the water cannons and focused solely on taking down that missile.

But still, I couldn't focus enough. I wasn't feeling enough

power. That crushing sensation that'd suffocated me ever since the mothership had arrived seemed to be gaining in strength. The sensation that Daniel said he felt, too.

The missile was just feet away.

I tried to create a wormhole.

I tried everything.

But then, in the end, it was worthless.

I was powerless.

I was—

"Good job I check the news," a voice said.

I looked over my shoulder.

Daniel was there.

He stopped the missile in its tracks.

Then, a second later, he teleported us away, back to our island base to ready ourselves for the attempt.

It took us four hours to fill the water cannons.

But when we were done, we positioned them toward the mothership, then shot up into the sky, so we were as close as we could safely get.

"We fire the water," Orion said. "Then we launch our attack."

"So again," Damon said. "We're just hoping for the best, basically?"

Saint nodded. "Basically."

We all looked up at the smooth exterior of the mothership and wondered whether this was really it. It felt like we were just going through the motions. But we'd spotted a weakness—an aversion—to water, and now we had to exploit it.

"Ready?" Stone asked. He was standing over the biggest of the water cannons.

I held my breath, and I nodded. "Ready."

I waited for the water to pound out of the cannons.

I waited for it to fire toward the mothership.

For a second, I wondered if something was going wrong.

Then a massive surge of water blasted out of the cannon toward the mothership.

I watched the thick stream of water fire out. Then I watched the rest of the water cannons begin to fire. I clenched my fists. I knew I had to be ready to attack the mothership. All of us did.

But still I shook.

Still, I didn't feel like I was strong enough for this.

And then, just when the water got closer to the mothership, something happened.

The water stopped.

We were silent, all of us, for a few seconds. We didn't want to believe that it was possible that something else wasn't working out, and was going wrong.

But it was.

"It's stopped," Cassie said.

I saw the color of the water changing. I saw it turning green. And I could see the steam coming off it.

Like it was hot.

Like it was...

"Acid," I said.

Damon turned to me. "What was that?"

My body filled with dread. My heart raced. "Acid. I said. It's acid!"

The others didn't realize right away. But by that point, it was too late.

The water, which had turned to acid, was hurtling back in our direction.

I lifted my hands to push it back, but then something else happened.

A massive tentacle reached out from above and dragged me away.

The Resistance were on their own.

I was captured.

[25]

I felt the grip tightening around my neck and I knew I didn't have long left.

All around me, there was darkness. Total darkness, so black it was suffocating. Just looking at that darkness made me feel a wave of sickness and light-headedness, in the way a young kid feared the dark at night. The same reason they begged their parents to keep a night light on for them. There were always monsters in the dark, in the mind of a kid.

Except right now, there really was a monster in this darkness.

The grip tightened even harder around my neck. I kicked back, reflexively more than anything. There was nothing else I could do, not really. I'd tried sparking my powers. I'd tried firing my way free of this mess. All of it was to no avail.

I was trapped. And the life was slipping away from me by the second.

I heard the blasts all around me, accompanied by the screams, and the feeling of sickness deep within grew even more intense. A bitter taste of blood and vomit filled my mouth, making me want to cough. I could smell something in the air. I couldn't describe it any other way than a thickness. Like the air was filled with tar, and that thickness was getting even more slimy, making breathing gradually more difficult.

But it was the eyes that scared me more than anything.

There was nothing grandiose about these eyes. There was nothing menacing about them, to the average person. It was their familiarity that got to me more than anything. I'd looked into these eyes before, a number of times. I'd stared into them, and they'd stared back at me.

And now they were the eyes that were looking at me as I struggled for my final breaths.

"It's over," the deep, gruff voice said. "Don't fight it. This is the only way it happens. This is the way it's always happened. Just... release."

I didn't want to stop fighting, as much as giving up any resistance would be the easy option here. So I gritted my teeth and kept my focus on those eyes, like I had so many times already. "N... never."

The hand around my neck loosened just enough for me to catch some breath. I coughed, then I felt vomit trickling up and out of my mouth, stilling my quest for a good lungful of air.

When I'd spewed up, the grip tightened once again, and I was pinned back hard against a solid wall.

As I was held there, I wondered what I had done to deserve this life. I was Kyle Peters. I wasn't even in my twenties, and yet somehow, I was the strongest ULTRA in existence—at least people thought, and at least people expected. I didn't *ask* to be Glacies. Glacies just became me.

I'd been dealt these cards and now I was being forced to live with them. Now, I was being forced to accept who I was. But also something else.

I was being forced to accept that I wasn't as strong as I'd hoped—or as the world hoped—all along.

"All these years of resisting instead of living," the voice said. "Now, it's time to stop. It's time to hand yourself over. So stop resisting, Kyle. End the pain. For yourself. For your family."

The mention of my family made me feel a warmth deep inside. But it was a warmth tinged with sadness. After all, my family had been torn apart, all because of me. It had been decimated, all because of me.

I felt a tear roll down my cheek when I thought of Ellicia, Dad, Damon, Avi, Cassie, Daniel, Orion, and all my old friends from the Resistance. "I can't stop fighting. For... for their sakes. I can't give up."

The figure chuckled, then. As he did, the room lit up, and I saw my surroundings for the first time in God-knows-how-long. I was in some kind of dark cavern. It was massive. It stretched as tall as I could see, and the walls were further away than I could perceive. The sheer size of this place was enough to make the hairs on my arms stand on end, purely because something this big wasn't human. It wasn't man-made. It was alien. Totally alien.

The scariest thing about it, though?

That bright light, shining right in the middle of this cavernous void.

And yet...

"I can't give up," I said. "And I won't give up."

I held my breath and thought of all the pain in my life. As I thought of the pain—and there was a lot of it, not least the pain I'd felt these last few days, some of the purest pain of all—I felt my powers getting stronger once again. I could feel them charging up. I could feel the ice creeping down my spine, stretching down my arms, scaling my fingers, tickling my fingertips.

I went to lift my arms and fire at the one holding me.

Their grip around my neck loosened completely. I felt my

stomach turn as I dropped down below. Immediately, I triggered my flight powers, needing to regain some sense of composure.

But nothing happened.

I was still falling.

I felt my stomach drop as I hurtled toward the ground. I shouted out and lifted my hands in the air, trying to fire some kind of ice to the roof of this cavern.

But the cavern walls and ceilings were just too high.

The ice didn't grip with the walls.

I kept on falling.

As I fell, fear filling my body, scrambling from side to side, for a moment, I felt a sense of calm. It was weird, and totally unexpected, but it was there.

Calm, because soon, there'd be nothing left of me.

Calm, because I wouldn't have to fight any longer.

And, ultimately, the position of not having to fight any longer was what I'd been striving toward all this time, right?

The cavern floor grew rapidly closer as I hurtled through the air toward it.

Sadness filled my body. I felt more tears roll down my cheeks, my throat wobbling. "I love you..." I started, intending to say "Mom" or "Dad" or "Ellicia" or anyone after it.

But in the end, there were so many people I loved that I couldn't say a thing.

I looked up. Above, I saw that total pitch black darkness again.

I felt the fear creeping up into my chest.

I held my breath.

Then, I fired one last shot of ice right up toward the ceiling.

I stopped.

Confusion filled my body. I spun left and right, still gasping in the darkness as I hovered there, totally static. *Did I do it? Did the ice stick?*

Then the face appeared in front of me all over again.

They were smiling, now.

Their smile made my body shake. I tried to look away, but I couldn't. It was like they had me wrapped up in some hypnotic trance.

They grabbed my neck again. I battled for that final breath. I didn't get a lungful.

"You should've given up when I gave you the opportunity," the voice said. "You were a fool for fighting. Now, we do things the hard way."

The figure stretched out their hand and pressed it against my chest.

Immediately, I felt a searing pain stretch through my body, and I lurched from side to side. "You won't win!" I shouted. "You'll never win!"

The figure smiled again, their hand still pressed against my chest. "That's where you're wrong, Kyle Peters. And this is where it ends for you, I'm afraid. It's been nice knowing you. But really, it's time."

The burning sensation in my chest spread right across my body. I tried to spark my powers, but the burning just seemed to melt my ice right away. I tried to teleport, but I couldn't. I was just too weak.

"You won't win," I shouted. "You won't..."

There was nothing else to say. I didn't even have the strength to speak now.

The figure pushed their hand further into my chest.

More pain.

More fear.

More weakness.

I saw a light blue glow illuminate in front of me, then. I felt sick right away. I knew what this was.

"You've already lost," the figure said, dragging the blue light from my body like they were taking away my innards. "Goodbye, Kyle Peters. Goodnight. This is where your story ends."

The last of the blue light was dragged from my body.

This is where your story ends...

I was starting to believe it, as my body gave up fighting, and darkness closed in.

I OPENED MY EYES, then, and I realized.

I was floating in the ocean. My skin was burning, sizzling. The rest of the Resistance were floating on beside me. It looked like I'd somehow managed to escape that tentacle that'd wrapped around me and pulled me from the sky. The big lumps of ice I could see around us must've been the acid. I must've frozen it at the very last.

But there was something I could remember, now.

Something I knew I'd been trying so hard to resist.

When I'd first defeated Catalyst, I'd blacked out. I'd stood beside Orion, Saint, and Daniel, and I'd watched the mothership get closer to me.

Only I'd seen who had been leading it.

I'd seen who the man was.

I'd seen the look in his eyes, and I knew who he was.

HIELO LOWERED his mask and looked into his reflection.

He looked at the scars on his face. The thinning of his hair. He looked at the protrusion of his ribs and the paling of his skin, all from his many years of fighting.

But more than anything, he looked at the ice on his palms. The first power he'd channeled. The power that, many eons ago, used to define who he was. The *hero* he was.

He looked at the ice and he remembered who he used to be.

"He's me," I muttered, drifting across the water, unable to believe what I was remembering.

Unable to believe what I'd seen when I'd looked into the mothership leader's eyes.

"The man. The man leading the mothership. He's... he's me."

[26]

I opened my eyes and right away, I understood the reality of my situation now.

I was back on the shore of one of the Galapagos islands we were using as our base. The sun was bright, but there was a cold chill in the air. I could taste sea salt on my dry lips, and my stomach churned for food.

But there were more important things than eating right now.

"Nice of you to wake up."

I turned onto my front and saw Vortex standing over me.

Behind her, I could see the rest of the Resistance. They looked battered and bruised, like this time they'd all been in serious conflict instead of just me. Which, as selfish as it sounded, kind of made things better, because at least I didn't look like a total idiot.

I struggled to my feet, my head spinning with the knowledge of what I'd just seen and discovered. "Let me guess. I started seizing again?"

"Not exactly," Vortex said. "This time, luckily for you, we all got thumped out of the sky by that tentacle. But yeah. You seemed to take it particularly badly. Mumbling things in your sleep. Good job Stone's around. He dragged you out of the water."

I looked over at Stone and gave him a thumbs up.

He gave me the middle finger.

I walked over to the rest of the Resistance, Vortex by my side. I knew I couldn't keep what I'd seen in my mind from them. Sure, it might just be in my mind as far as they were concerned. But I knew there was something more to what I'd seen. Something totally *real*.

Orion put a hand on my shoulder when I reached him, patting it. "Good to see you awake again."

"And you. Everyone okay?"

"A few cuts and bruises, here and there. But mostly positive."

I looked around at the circle of Resistance standing in front of me. I felt the nerves kicking in, my heart racing. But I had to be open. I had to be honest.

"I know something about the mothership. The leader of the mothership."

Everyone stopped their chatting to one another and looked right at me.

"This isn't gonna be another one of your weird dreams is it, bro?" Daniel asked.

I knew then that this wasn't going to be easy. "I might've seen it. But I know for a fact it's real, now."

"What's real?" Cassie asked.

I looked at her, and then I looked at Saint, and the rest of the group. I had to be honest. I had to be frank. "The leader of the mothership. The one who spoke to us and told us he was hunting the ULTRAs down. It's... it's me."

I saw the frowns. I heard the baffled gasps.

"What?" Daniel asked.

"I know it sounds mad."

"Yeah," Stone said. "It sounds like the ramblings of a lunatic."

"But you have to believe me. I mean, me even being here right now is not *right*. There's so much weirdness and so much wrong. This would just be the next in a long line."

Roadrunner shook her head. She was nursing a wound on her ankle. "But I don't actually understand. What do you *mean* it's you?"

I pictured myself staring back at me, those unmistakable eyes. "I don't know how, but there's some kind of... of alternate, parallel reality, or something. A reality where I want to take out the ULTRAs on this planet—including myself—for whatever reason."

Stone opened his mouth and laughed. For the first time in a long time, he sounded genuinely amused. "No. Look. What you're saying, kid. It's insane. Completely crazy."

"I know it sounds it. But it's the truth. And it leaves me with a choice."

"And that choice is?"

I scratched the back of my neck. I hadn't even faced up to the choice myself yet, or the ramifications of what it meant. But I could see the decision clearly ahead of me.

Make headway and act on my knowledge, as much as I didn't believe I was strong enough?

Or to keep on running away and fighting the inevitable?

"It's too late for me to keep on running. That isn't going to get me or any of us anywhere anymore."

"So what do you suggest?" Stone asked. "Saying we do decide to believe you. What's the plan?"

I looked at Stone, Vortex, and Roadrunner and I saw doubt.

But the others. All the others. Damon. Saint. Orion. Cassie. Daniel. In their eyes, I saw belief.

I took a deep breath, and for the first time, I faced up to what was inevitable.

"I'll only be able to defeat myself if I discover my own weaknesses," I said. "And if I believe I'm strong enough to win."

"And do you?" Stone asked.

I didn't answer that.

Honestly, I wasn't sure I did. Not yet.

But I was about to find out whether I was strong enough after all.

[27]

I held my breath and braced myself for a challenge I wasn't sure I was ready to take on.

I was in the middle of the Colombian rainforest, right in the Darién Gap. The Darién Gap is generally renowned as one of the most dangerous places on Earth. It's the one area where, if you're traveling down from the top of North America right through to South America, the road totally stops, and gives way to jungle. Inside that jungle? Mercenaries. Dangerous wildlife. And since the proliferation of the ULTRAs, lots of ULTRA-rebels, too, misusing their powers and abilities.

But I wasn't worried about wildlife or mercenaries right now.

I looked at the trees surrounding me. They were tall and suffocating, their greenness so bright that they burned my eyes.

Everywhere around me, I could hear the noise from a different creature. Insects. Frogs. Birds. A cocktail of life, which would typically be so beautiful. But it was so loud that it was actually disorienting.

I had to keep my focus. I had to make sure I was totally

committed to fighting, or I wouldn't discover what my true weaknesses were.

Because I could be sure as hell that Alternate Kyle—as I was now dubbing him—wasn't going to be slacking when it came to the final showdown.

I walked slowly through the leaves, which crunched underfoot. The insects flew into me, which I swatted away. I wasn't wearing my Glacies gear, which made me feel even more exposed. It was a suggestion of Vortex's. The Glacies gear was something of a shield to me. Even if it was mostly psychological, I still felt much stronger when I was wearing it.

But right now, I just had to be myself. As strong as I could possibly be without any costumes for mental resolve.

I needed to find out whether I was capable of defeating myself.

I saw rustling in the leaves up ahead.

My heart picked up. I tensed my fists and walked toward it.

The closer I got, I saw that rustling again. There was a definite movement there. Perhaps an animal. A wild pig, or something like that.

Or perhaps...

When I got within inches of the movement, I heard something directly above.

I looked up.

Stone was clinging to a tree right above me.

"Boo," he said.

Then he came flying down at me, rocky fist extended.

For a split second, I felt a twinge of fear, like I had to hold back because this was just Stone, and it was all just a test of my strengths.

But then I knew I wouldn't be giving a real account of myself if I didn't fight back as hard as I could.

Stone got closer to me. His fist pulled back.

I lifted my hands and fired a blast of ice at him. I didn't hold back.

The ice smacked into him, pushing him upwards and giving me time to maneuver.

I swung to my right, readied myself to send Stone into a wormhole in the ground, which would teleport him to somewhere like New Zealand.

And then I felt a smack across my face and I went flying onto my ass.

My cheek ached like mad. I lay there for a few seconds, dazed, not really sure of what'd happened.

Then I saw the blurring hovering around above me.

"Roadrunner," I muttered.

She flew into me a few more times, smacking me in the head, chest, and stomach. Part of me was surprised at how much she was throwing at me. But then, that's what I'd asked for. I couldn't truly be tested if everyone was going easy on me.

I raised my hands instinctively, trying to wade off Roadrunner's attacks.

That did no good. She just knocked my hands down, battering and bruising me.

In the corner of my eye, I could see Stone standing. He was getting closer to me.

Come on, Kyle. You're stronger than these two. You're the strongest ULTRA ever to have lived.

I lifted a hand and pushed a ball of energy in Roadrunner's direction.

The attacks stopped.

Time went still, just for a second.

The sky above went completely dark.

Then I opened up a spiraling wormhole, which dragged Stone and Roadrunner toward it.

"Sorry," I said, half-smiling at Stone as he disappeared into the abyss.

He shook his head. "Oh, you will be."

Then the wormhole slammed shut, and the pair of them were gone.

I put my hands on my knees and took a few gasps for air. Two down. Just... shit. Six to go.

Six left, and I hadn't even had to take on Orion or Saint yet.

I lifted myself upright and I saw Damon standing opposite me.

He had his fists raised. Purple electricity flickered across them.

"Come on then," he said. "Bring it on."

I smirked. Laughed a little.

Then I clicked my fingers and sent Damon flying up into the sky, screaming.

It was when Damon disappeared that I felt a presence behind me.

Then something tightened around my neck.

The pain was intense. Far greater than any pain I'd felt in this showdown up to now. I knew without looking that it was one of the big three. Orion, Saint, Daniel.

And I knew from the intensity of the pain that it couldn't be Orion. And that it probably wasn't going to be Daniel, either.

I spun around.

Saint was standing over me.

He had a hand raised. He was slowly tightening it, suffocating me.

He lifted me into the air. All of a sudden, this didn't feel like sparring anymore. I kicked my feet out. I was going to die here. He was going to kill me.

"You know, you look so weak, without your costume," he said. "So... helpless."

I clutched at the invisible hands around my throat. I could feel my skin going cold, my eyes bulging out of my skull.

"I'm starting to think I should just finish you right here so the world's all mine. What will the world do without Glacies? What will the world do without poor Kyle Peters?"

My vision blurred. I could feel myself drifting off into oblivion. My muscles were weakening, and my ability to fight was waning.

"What will the world do without its great savior?" Saint asked. "What will Ellicia do when there's no one home to protect her?"

"Saint!"

I heard the voice from behind Saint and saw someone running through the trees. Orion and Cassie.

But Saint didn't stop.

"What will the world do when I kill them all?"

Cassie threw herself at Saint. "Saint, stop!"

But he didn't.

Instead, he lifted a finger and sliced her in half.

I felt myself screaming even though my throat was being crushed.

After that, I saw Orion fall to his knees, blood spilling out of his chest.

I saw Damon breaking his bones.

Stone's arm being chipped away.

I saw everything falling apart.

"What will you do now, Kyle?" Saint asked.

"Please!" I begged. There was nothing else I could do. "Please."

I saw Saint smile.

Then I dropped to the ground and suddenly, everything went bright again.

I lay there for a few seconds. I felt sick. Totally sick after having just witnessed the slaughter of the Resistance. I should've known Saint was still evil. I'd fallen for it, and now they were gone.

"Kyle?"

I looked to my left, and my muscles loosened.

Cassie was standing there.

By her side, Damon.

And by his side...

"Vortex," I said.

I covered my head with my hands. I understood now. The whole incident with Saint hadn't been real. It'd been a Vortex driven illusion, after all.

"You're shaking," Vortex said. She smiled. "Did I scare the shit out of you?"

I nodded. "Something like that."

"Which is a good thing," Saint said, walking to the fore. "Because we know what your weakness is now."

I nodded and attempted a smile, but to be honest, I felt so broken down by what I'd just witnessed. I didn't know if I had it in me to try again.

"Your biggest weakness is your mind," Orion said. "So now we get to work on making *you* mentally stronger, so you can mentally exploit your enemy. Yourself."

My stomach sank. "And that means?"

Orion looked at Vortex, who tensed her fists and started rolling her eyes back into her skull. "We get back to work. Scaredy-cat."

It was horrifying. It was going to be all kinds of nasty.

But at least I knew what I had to do, now.

[28]

Hielo watched the showdown unfolding in the jungle from afar.

He wasn't there, exactly. But of course, he was once Kyle Peters, so he had the ability to be somewhere without exactly being there. Besides, he was much older and much more experienced than the Kyle down there right now, fighting on earth.

He watched him with curiosity, though. He tried to keep himself as detached from Kyle as possible, but he couldn't help feeling like he *was* that boy down there, trying his best to hone his abilities, to fight the good fight.

And although he knew that was him exactly once upon a time, it wasn't him. Not really. Hielo had changed a lot since that day all those years ago. He'd seen how the world had changed. He'd seen what had happened, the changes, the developments. And he knew when he saw all the changes that had unfolded, that he wasn't the same person.

And that what he was doing right now was right. Completely right.

He heard a whirring above, which distracted him from

watching Kyle and the others sparring. He looked up and saw the bright beam of energy reaching down into another batch of ULTRAs, harvesting their abilities and using them for himself.

Because the abilities they'd harvested were a part of the real plan.

And the real plan was...

He saw it, then.

He saw the pain Kyle had felt.

He saw the weakness. The images.

Saint, destroying Cassie, then Damon, then the rest of his friends.

He saw these flashes and then he knew. As if he'd never known at all, it came to him.

His weakness was his thoughts.

His mental resilience—or lack of it—was where he fell down.

Of course it was.

Kyle Peters, aged nineteen, still didn't believe in his own strengths, his own abilities. One day, he would. He'd find the strength and the courage to *be* the person Hielo was right now.

But right now, he was but a fraction of what he was destined to become.

And that's why Hielo was here.

To make sure he never, ever became as powerful as he had the potential of being.

Because he knew what came with that power.

"We've got eyes on Kyle," a voice to his right said. It was B8384, another of his soldiers. "Would you like us to proceed with our attack?"

Hielo gritted his teeth, a habit he'd always had in times of stress. He held his breath and saw Kyle thinking he was getting stronger and stronger, having no idea of what was ahead of him, of what was to come.

"We wait. He's almost ready to attack. And when he does... we hit him right where it hurts."

"And where's that?"

Hielo smiled.

He knew exactly how to hurt Kyle.

[29]

It was a few hours later that I found Ellicia and Avi again.

They had been sent to a camp just outside of Maryland state. It was pretty well-located, out of the way of most of the major towns and cities. The way these camps had been set up was well thought out, too. There weren't too many people in any one place. That was just asking for trouble. At the camp Ellicia and Avi were in, there were just a thousand people. A fair few, but not enough to make anyone place susceptible to attack for any particular reason.

I'd come here because I needed to see my girlfriend and my friend before everything changed.

I'd come here because I was taking the fight to Alternate Kyle—as I was now calling him—and I knew it might well be my last fight.

The sun had set, but the grounds were still filled with guards. They were armed to the max, mostly in anti-ULTRA gear and guns. I knew there would be fences erected around the camp to deter ULTRAs. But fortunately for me, I wasn't just any old ULTRA.

I slipped inside and made my way, invisibly, along the aisles.

I knew Ellicia and Avi were here because I'd managed to hack into and track down the manifesto. The further I walked, the more nervous I grew that maybe I'd got this all wrong, and that maybe they weren't here at all. Perhaps something bad had happened to them. I didn't want to think about that, but it was an option I had to consider.

I was about to turn around and start my search again when I saw her sitting on the edge of her bed.

My body felt like it was melting the moment I laid eyes on her. And not just because she was there, with her long brown hair, and with those big blue eyes. But because of who else was with her.

Avi.

But also, Dad.

"Hi," I said.

They all spun around in unison, like I'd taken them by surprise.

Then all of their faces dropped, and they ran toward me, Dad first.

"Kyle," he said.

He grabbed hold of me and started crying. I couldn't resist my tears either, as Ellicia and Avi joined in the hug.

"It's okay," I said. "I'm here. I'm—"

"We thought you were dead."

I nodded, instantly feeling guilty that I hadn't taken the time to reunite with Dad since I'd returned to... well, to life. "I know. And I'm sorry. I just..."

"You don't have to be sorry," Dad said, squeezing me tighter. "You're here now. That's what matters."

I bonded with Dad, Ellicia, and Avi a little more after that. We spoke about normal things like the state of the world before I'd come back to consciousness, the things I'd missed. Rubbish television, and the like.

And then we got on to the real reason I was here.

"So this spaceship," Dad said, "or whatever it is. I'm guessing you're onto it, in some way."

I didn't want to tell anyone else about who was fronting the mothership. So I just nodded. "Yeah. Something like that."

"And you'll be able to stop it," Ellicia said, tightening her grip around my hand. "You'll be able to defeat it. Won't you?"

I didn't tighten my grip around her hand in turn. I just sat there, uncertain about everything.

But I had to believe.

I had to believe or there was no way I'd succeed.

"I'm going to do the best I can," I said.

Dad smiled. "That's my boy."

The small talk kicked in again. But it wasn't long before I was dragging the conversation back to the real reason I was here.

I fidgeted with my cuffs, turning invisible every time a guard walked by or someone poked their head around the door. "What I have to do. You have to understand it's dangerous. So dangerous. And I can't... I can't put you in any more danger."

Avi narrowed his eyes. "What's that mean?"

"It means I'm not sure I'll... I'm not sure I'll..."

I couldn't finish what I was trying to say: that I wasn't sure if I'd ever see them again.

But Dad put a hand on my arm. Then Ellicia did, then Avi.

I looked into their eyes and I saw that they all understood.

"We know," Avi said. "We get it, bro. But we got faith in you. All of us got faith in you."

I hugged them again, and as their warmth radiated through my body, it really felt like we were holding each other for the last time.

Then I got up, walked over to the door, and looked back at them.

"I love you," I said, my voice cracking. "All of you."

And they all looked back at me, smiling. "We love you too," Ellicia said. "Now go save the world."

I wiped a tear away from my face.

Then I took a deep breath, focused all my energy on this loving, painful moment, and I teleported away.

It was time to go after Alternate Kyle before he caused any more destruction.

It was time to stop reacting.

It was time to start attacking.

[30]

It was time.

The sun was just about rising, but it didn't matter up here, way in the sky. The closer we got to the outer atmosphere of the earth, the darker it got, regardless of how much closer to the sun we were. There was a difference to the sun when you were within the Earth's atmosphere and the sun when you were just outside it. When you were on Earth, there was still something mystical about it like it really was just a flat light there to illuminate your day.

But when you were outside the confines of the atmosphere, it really took on its true, three-dimensional form.

So too did Alternate Kyle's mothership.

I looked around at the people flying with me. It was the bedrock of the Resistance, as the Resistance stood in its current form—Orion, Daniel, Saint, Cassie, Damon, Roadrunner, Vortex, Stone. All of us were united, all of us with one common goal: to try and use what we'd learned about my own weaknesses to take down Alternate Kyle.

And it was clear where my real weaknesses were. It was clear to everybody what my real weaknesses were.

Mental weaknesses.

I didn't believe in myself enough.

I had to use those mental images to exploit my lack of belief and defeat my alternate self.

And at the forefront of that was Vortex.

Up ahead, I saw the mothership. There was an opening right at the bottom of it, where the crafts came out of.

"Is that the way we're heading in?" Vortex asked.

I nodded. "You sure you're up to this?"

She smiled back at me. "Kyle, I saw you peeing your pants when I got inside your head. I've seen it again and again. I know *exactly* what'll trigger you—if all this crap about this being an alternate version of yourself is true, anyway. Trust me. I've got this."

I felt more anxious when Vortex responded with such confidence. I knew this wasn't going to be an easy fight. There was a sense inside me that told me a lot of misery and a lot of drama was ahead.

And yet, there was nothing I could do to act on that knowledge, 'cause it was so vague and formless.

All I could do was attack.

I turned around to the rest of the Resistance. All of them stopped and looked at me, waiting for further command.

"Okay," I said. "Here's what we do. We get to the exterior vent, where the crafts are ejected. I create a wormhole big enough to swallow them up. Stone, you bash any spares into space. Cassie and Damon, fry their electrics. Roadrunner, you lead them into these traps. And Orion, Saint, Daniel... you know what you do. What you do best."

All of them nodded at that.

"And Vortex," I said, looking to her. "You make your way inside. You find Alternate Kyle. You paralyze him with thoughts."

"And then you finish the job," she said.

It sounded so simple. Too simple. And I couldn't possibly know how un-simple or how much of a struggle it was going to be just yet.

"Hold up," Damon said. "Looks like we've got company."

In the distance, from the belly of the mothership, a crowd of crafts spurted out. There were lots of them. Ten. Then twenty. Then thirty.

I lifted my hands and tensed them, ice spreading across them.

"You sure you've got this?" Cassie asked.

I pressed my teeth together. "I'm sure," I said.

Then I powered in the direction of the mothership.

"Let's go!"

The battle started right away. The crafts were on us within seconds. Three of them flew at me, swinging their tentacles in my direction, trying to slice and cut at me.

But I just fired ice back at each and every one of them that attempted to stop me, flowing between them like water. I felt much more confident about myself, now. Like I had my strength and belief back, and everything was working out just as it should.

Up at the mothership, I saw more of those crafts falling out. Tension kicked in and made my stomach tingle. I needed to get up there fast and create that wormhole. Creating wormholes took a lot of energy, so I needed time to do it. I wasn't going to do it if I was swarmed by these crafts.

"Cassie," I shouted.

Two of the crafts flew at her.

Stone knocked one of them away, while Cassie fried the next one with her electricity. She looked over at me like I was an unwanted distraction right now. "A little busy, brother!"

"I need you to hold them off here instead," I said.

She frowned, as another of the crafts made its way toward her. "What?"

I looked back up at the mothership. Crafts were still bursting out of it. "There's not going to be enough time. I need to activate the wormhole right now."

"But—"

"Just hold them off, okay? I won't be long. Trust me."

We made eye contact, just for a split second, and I could see the doubt she had.

Then she nodded and carried on with her fighting.

I looked back up at that mothership. The crafts weren't slowing down in their ejection. I needed to create a wormhole big enough to drag them all down it. But doing so wasn't going to be easy. I'd never built a wormhole anywhere near that big before.

Just then, I saw movement in the corner of my eye. I jolted around and saw another five crafts speeding toward me, ambushing me from the side.

I fired immediately at each of them, making every blast of ice stronger and more energized than the last.

But then I saw the crafts heading to my left, and I soon realized what was happening. The crafts weren't flying at the rest of the Resistance anymore. They were heading to me, and only to me.

This must've been part of the plan all along.

Whatever plan Alternate Kyle had for me, whatever game he was playing, he was clearly targeting me right now.

I wasn't going to stand for it.

I forged an ice shield with each of my hands, as strong as I could.

The first of the crafts slammed into it, smashing into pieces.

Then more hit it, and I felt my arms caving in, my shields weakening, as one after the other hit and hit and hit.

My arms went totally weak then, and before I knew it, my ice shields were shattered and down completely.

The crafts were speeding toward me.

They were just inches away.

They were going to take me down, all over again...

Then I thought about the painful things I'd seen when Vortex had got inside my head, and instead of letting them weaken me, I let them strengthen me.

"No," I said.

A craft flew at my face.

I lifted my hand and stretched out my fingers.

The craft stopped.

It hovered in midair. More of the crafts flew at me, but all of these went still, too. In no time at all, I was completely surrounded by these crafts, all of them blocking my vision outside.

I felt warmth in the middle of my chest, and I knew the feeling and what it was now. I didn't understand it, not completely. But that warmth was like a vibration. It was making me feel stronger and more powerful, and more energized.

I can do this.

The crafts started to drift further back, gradually, one at a time.

I can do this!

I clenched my fists together.

What happened next amazed even me.

The crafts were there one second.

The next, they disintegrated, disappearing into nothing but fine pieces of dust.

I looked at the dust cloud that was on the crafts in awe. My breathing raced, with what little oxygen was left up here. I'd just made the crafts vanish like they were nothing. I'd just disintegrated them, one by one.

"Glacies," Vortex called. "There's an opening. This is our chance."

I looked up and saw what she meant.

There were no more crafts coming out of the mothership.

The mothership was gearing up to drift off into the distance.

It had to be now.

I tightened my focus and headed in the direction of the mothership, Vortex by my side. This was the moment things turned. This was the moment we started winning. This was the—

First, a splitting headache.

Then, images of my family, my friends, of everyone I'd ever known and loved falling.

Then, paralysis.

I floated there in the sky, totally still, and tried to shake free of the invisible grip that had me in its clutches.

But nothing could break me free.

Then I saw something else.

Vortex was paralyzed, too.

She was in the grip of whatever I was.

Only she was being dragged up toward the mothership, away from me, away from everyone.

"Vortex!" Stone shouted.

He tried to fly in her direction to save her, but he hit an invisible wall.

She got further away.

I pushed even harder, resisting the pull of the mothership. I shook, twisted, and turned, and eventually, using all the energy I had, I managed to shake free of whatever this grip was.

"Vortex! We have to go after her, kid. We have to get her!"

But as I looked up at the mothership, which was disappearing into the distance, I saw already that it was too late.

One second, Vortex was there.
The next, she was gone.

[31]

Vortex opened her eyes and right away, she knew she was in danger.

She was pinned down to some kind of table. Above her, there was an opening, that stretched upwards for what seemed like miles. She could taste blood on her lips, and there was a dizziness to her head that she could only describe as similar to waking up after being under anesthetic.

She used to be terrified of falling to sleep, right from a young age, because of the nightmares. Her parents weren't concerned, not in the early days. They told her it was a phase that she'd grow out of.

But she didn't grow out of it. And when she finally hit nine years old, it was then that her parents accepted that something was horribly wrong. They were exhausted. They didn't know what to do.

Then Vortex had gone in for an MRI scan, and the doctors had found something wrong with her brain. They hadn't been able to identify what it was exactly. It wasn't a tumor. More... a shadow. An unidentified darkness. It wasn't long before they were operating on her, and she was under general anesthetic, her parents waiting to find out whether their daughter was ever going to return to them again.

Then, a funny thing happened.

Soon after they'd identified that shadow, all three of the lead doctors that had been working on Vortex's case had killed themselves.

Again, nobody really thought much of it. It was a coincidence, and nothing more.

But Vortex always felt like she was involved, somehow. Like she was responsible.

That's because she hadn't been totally unconscious when she'd been under anesthetic.

She remembered seeing the three men poking around her skull and she'd bitten back against them. She'd got into their minds, made them imagine all kinds of ugly, horrible thoughts.

She'd haunted them, as far as Vortex was concerned. And that haunting had led to their suicide.

It was in the years after that which Vortex really started to hone her skills, and realized she was, in fact, an ULTRA, and she had a very powerful ability—the power to get inside people's minds and haunt their thoughts.

But as she lay there, trying to wriggle free of the bands wrapped around her body, Vortex felt weak. She felt like she couldn't use any powers at all. Of course, by default, being an ULTRA gave her the ability to levitate. Eight out of ten ULTRAs were gifted with the same abilities. Levitation wasn't something that just crept up on you, though. It was something you realized whether you had it or not very suddenly, like if you fall from a height or see a car speeding toward you.

Vortex's discovery of levitation had been the latter, when a jealous ex-boyfriend, Riley, whose thoughts she'd haunted decided he'd had enough of both his life and hers.

She jumped inhumanly out of his way.

He'd gone crashing into a wall.

Levitation was never an easy thing for Vortex to trigger, though. Some ULTRAs had it better than others.

Then there had been the jarring realization of what she was and what that made her in the eyes of the people and the government. There'd been some hard times.

But she'd found the Resistance. And then she'd found Glacies. And Stone.

Since then, life had been much better.

She heard footsteps approaching her. She seized up, trying to activate her abilities but unable to.

The footsteps walked around the side of the metal bed—or slab—and stopped right by her side.

She hesitated for a few moments before looking. She didn't want to see who it was. She didn't want to face reality. At least, not the reality that Kyle had told her about.

When she looked at the figure at her bedside, she could have no doubts.

"Vortex," the figure—Alternate Kyle—said. "Long time no see."

Vortex felt tears filling up in her eyes. This man might be old, with pale, wrinkled skin, narrowed cheekbones, and a frail body. He might be dressed in black now, and hooded. But there was no doubting that this was Kyle. "Glacies."

"Oh, please," he said. "I prefer Hielo now. It's Spanish for ice. A rebranding, if you will."

He smiled, and Vortex saw the Kyle she'd had a crush on ever since she'd first met him in that smile. That's what haunted her about it. There was no denying who this was.

And yet he had her tied down here, staring up into some kind of endless abyss.

"Now, I know this isn't exactly the ideal surroundings for a reunion. But unfortunately, it's the only surroundings we've got.

How are you? How have you been keeping?" He paused then. Looked down at the ground. "No. Of course. You *aren't* the Vortex I knew. You're just a past life. You've already lived your life, you see. A long and great life. And please be assured that you play no part in what happens many, many years into the future. Your hands are clean of blood."

He put a hand on her chest.

"But that doesn't mean you're exempt from this."

Vortex swallowed. Her throat was so dry, and she felt so weak. "Please, Kyle. We're—we're your friends. Wherever you're from, whatever you think you're doing, we're the Res—"

"The Resistance," he spat. He smiled then, a speck of spit on the side of his chin. "That's what we called ourselves, wasn't it? The Resistance. Little did we know how the Resistance would turn out. Little did we know how much that we were on the wrong track. Because the truth? You want the truth about all this? About everything?"

He leaned into Vortex's ear, and he told her.

Everything, right from the beginning, right through the ages, and right to this moment, right now.

After he'd spoke, he stepped back. Vortex felt heavier, somehow. Like there was guilt inside her for what Kyle—Hielo—had told her.

Was it true?

Could it be true?

Were they really so responsible for everything Hielo had said?

And if so, was what he had planned really so wrong after all?

"Vortex," he said, his voice cracking as he elevated his hands over her body. "For what's next. For what I have to do. I am sorry. Really. And I... I know you'll believe me. After hearing what I've had to say."

Tears streamed down Vortex's cheeks. She shook her head, tried to fight, but all she could do was beg. "Please, Kyle. Please."

He looked away then. She could see he was tearing up, too.

Then he took in a sharp inhalation of breath and patted her on the stomach, snapping back into the detached self he'd become. "Right. We'd better get started."

He walked away, and the lights in the room went out.

All except for one.

It was directly above her, spiraling its way down that tunnel above, down toward her. It looked formless, but it was snakelike in its movement. It wasn't anything like *anything* that had been invented on Earth.

Not yet.

"Please," she said.

She kicked. She twisted. She gripped her fists together to fight free.

The light moved out of the mouth of the tunnel and hovered right over her face.

"Kyle. Kyle. Please."

She saw him making eye contact with her. And just for a fraction of a second, she swore she saw regret in his eyes. She swore she saw pain.

And then he turned away.

And after that, she didn't see anything.

The light slammed into her chest.

Her eyes squeezed shut.

And as Vortex's powers were sucked dry from her body, she started to scream.

[32]

I watched as the mothership disappeared into the distance and I didn't want to give up anymore. I wanted to fight.

The invisible shield that was blocking our assault on the mothership was still in place. No matter how much I or any of the other seven remaining members of the Resistance pushed and slammed against it, they just couldn't break through. The crafts had stopped flying out of the mothership, but they didn't need to be. Not anymore.

All that was needed was this glass barrier.

All that was needed was our knowledge that Vortex had been taken.

I looked around and saw Stone still slamming into that invisible barrier. He was hitting it so hard that he was bleeding. His eyes were only focused on one thing—that mothership.

"Stone," I said. I floated over to his side.

He kept on slamming into the invisible shield. "I have to get to Vortex. I can't give up."

I felt so bad for him. I reached over for him. "Stone, we... we can't. She's—"

"No!"

He swung around and punched me, hard. The punch stung like mad, but I was able to steady myself. I could feel blood seeping down from my right eyebrow. I was dizzy.

But I couldn't blame Stone.

He loved Vortex. Just like I loved people myself.

And now Vortex was gone, and I was trying to tell him just to give up?

He kept on slamming against it, hitting it with his rock arm and his head until eventually, his attacks slowed down to a halt, and he hovered there, crying. Roadrunner went to his side, comforting him. They held each other, and they cried.

"What now?"

I looked to my right. Orion was standing there. Some of the others were listening, too.

I felt my skin tingling. "I don't know," I said. "How about you come up with some suggestions for once?"

Orion didn't seem fazed by my words. "Kyle, I'm sorry. Of course I'm sorry. But we have to make a call here."

I looked at the mothership in the distance and I knew what the call was. We could continue our attack against Alternate Kyle, or we could just give up.

Giving up seemed like the easiest option right now. I didn't want to lose anyone else. None of us did.

But that wasn't in our nature.

We were fighters.

I floated over to Stone's side. This time, I put a hand on his back, but it was a solid hand. Not in a patronizing manner.

He looked up at me, into my eyes.

"I won't give up," he said. "Not until I find her."

I nodded. "I'm not asking you to."

I turned to face the rest of the Resistance.

"I know it seems impossible right now. But we can't give up

our fight. If anything, this gives us even more of a reason to carry on."

They all hovered around me looking exhausted, defeated.

I couldn't let them give in.

"The only thing we can do is fight. Because we don't give up. That's not what we do."

"So what do you suggest?" Damon asked.

I looked him in the eyes. Then at the others, one by one. "We're going to clean our wounds. We're going to take a breather. And then we're going to intensify the fight."

"But Vortex," Cassie said. "You need her. She was a part of the plan. You aren't strong enough without her."

I nodded and looked up at the mothership. "That's why we're going to get her back."

"And if we don't?" Daniel asked.

I took a deep breath and hovered above the rest of the Resistance. "Then I'll die trying."

[33]

We all linked hands, and held our breath and readied ourselves to fly toward the invisible shield as the mothership disappeared into the distance.

"Ready?" I shouted.

Cassie nodded. Saint nodded. Everyone nodded. "Ready," they called.

I turned back to the invisible shield, and to the mothership. I tightened my grip around Stone's hand. "Good."

Then together, we flew in the direction of that invisible shield with as much force as possible.

I felt it smack against me and knock me back. It wasn't like a solid object exactly. More like a stretching form which was trying to keep us from moving past it.

But I could feel it shifting.

I could feel us breaking through.

I could feel...

We jolted back, all of us.

Electricity sparked across that invisible wall.

We were still on the wrong side of it.

"Shit," Stone said. He flew at the shield again and punched it some more. "Goddamned shield!"

"Can't we just teleport through it?" Damon asked.

I shook my head. "If we could, I'd have thought of that already. But no. The shield just blocks my teleportation, too. It's kind of like an—"

"Invisible net," Roadrunner said. "Right. You've only told us eighteen times already."

I felt my cheeks blushing a little. Then I looked back at that mothership, right in the distance. I thought about Vortex, who would be on board. I thought about what might be happening to her. I didn't *know* for certain, but there had been lucidity to the dreams I'd had when I'd been inside that mothership and watched a long arm of energy reach down and drag the powers from Rhynart's body.

I didn't want Vortex to suffer the same fate. I wasn't going to let that happen.

I might not have my Glacies gear on, but I didn't need it. Deep down inside, I was still Glacies. That was what mattered. That was what counted.

"I'm going to try something else," I said.

"Oh," Stone muttered. "You tell us that now."

"Just... just bear with me. Be patient. Please."

"What is it you're doing?"

I lifted my hands and steadied my focus on that mothership. "I'm not entirely sure yet."

"Well, that's just dandy."

"Please. Just have patience. I can do this."

I focused, then, on the tingling sensation I'd felt in my chest and right across my body when I'd rolled back time—however I'd done it. It was the same deep, rich energy that I'd used to fight off so many of those crafts in just a matter of seconds. I didn't know how to activate it on call. It seemed to just come to life in times of great need.

But right now, I could feel myself getting closer and closer to that tingling sensation, and I knew I needed to embrace it.

I heard voices behind me. Mumbles of confusion and bafflement at what I was doing.

In my mind's eye, I saw the mothership.

I saw myself getting closer to it.

I saw all of us getting closer to it.

The further we got to it, the more my skin started to burn.

I loosened my focus, then.

The mothership slipped back into the distance.

"Kyle?" It was Saint. "I appreciate your desire to help, here. But I can't see what good floating there and—"

"Shut up."

And he did. Chain of command duly noted.

I closed my eyes again and saw the mothership edging closer. I felt the vibrations in my body moving up my toes, my ankles, then up my legs to my knees, up my torso, right through my neck, all around my head. Before I knew it, every single fragment of my body was shaking with these violent, burning vibrations.

I felt the pain kicking in again. It intensified to a point where I wasn't sure I was going to be able to hold on.

But we were getting closer to that mothership again.

The closer we got, the more intense the burning felt.

I felt like I was being submerged in that lava from the bottom of Krakatoa.

I felt like I was bathing in the fires of the sun.

And still, I forced myself onwards.

Still, I got within inches of the mothership, my heart racing, my body shaking, my—

"Holy shit!"

The voice—Damon's—distracted me from my trance. The pain receded. The mothership disappeared from my mind. Everything was back to normal.

My face was on fire, not with the burning I'd felt anymore, but with rage at Damon for interrupting my flow. I spun around and squared up to him. "What the hell don't you understand about 'shut up,' man?"

Damon blinked, his wide eyes jolting from my face to behind me. He looked sheepish about something.

"Hey," I said. "I asked you a question."

"Kyle," Cassie said.

"No. No, you don't have to get involved here. Damon, I'm—"

"Kyle!"

When Cassie shouted, I saw that she was looking right behind me, then.

As was everyone else.

I didn't understand. "What..."

When I turned, I saw exactly what they were looking at.

The mothership was just inches away.

The opening that the crafts flew out of was right in front of us.

Their exit.

Our entrance.

"I did it," I mumbled.

Daniel patted me on the back. "Looks like whatever you did, you did something right."

He flew past me, left me there, jaw agape. "I did it..."

I felt confident, all of a sudden. Like I'd been granted a new lease of life. After all, I'd managed to tap into those mysterious, strong energies I didn't understand. I'd focused and I'd used them for my own gain. Previously, they'd been reactionary. But not anymore. I'd channeled those energies. If I could do that continually, then surely the channeling would get easier.

And if it got easier...

What exactly would I *not* be capable of?

The image of my impending strength both excited and terrified me.

But I wasn't left to mull over the future for much longer.

Out of the mothership, crafts started spilling out, one by one until there were more than the mind could perceive.

We backed up.

A whole wall of them blocked the entrance to the mothership, all of them focused on us.

"What now?" Damon asked.

I held my breath.

Tensed my fists.

"We fight."

[34]

Avi heard the noise outside his room and he knew right away that something was wrong.

It was night. Late at night. Usually, he was used to hearing a few whispers and a few snivels at night. After all, he was staying in a camp that had been designed to temporarily house those in vulnerable regions while the mothership commenced its attack on the ULTRAs. Of course people weren't just going to be quiet all the time. Sometimes, they were going to be goddamned noisy. That was just something you learned to live with.

Living in noisy conditions wasn't exactly new to Avi, either. He'd grown up in some pretty rough conditions. His mom—birth mom—had been an alcoholic. Sometimes they slept on the streets. Others, inside buildings that weren't much better.

Avi had grown used to falling asleep to the sound of traffic and people, right from an early age.

But this noise was different.

He stood up and walked over to the door to his room.

He looked outside at all the other doors. Really, it made his skin crawl, because they were just like prison cells. That said, elements of it were much more relaxed. There was an advisory curfew in place after eleven p.m., but that didn't mean you couldn't leave your room. You just had to be as quiet as possible if you were heading to the bathroom or whatever.

So it wasn't quite a prison. The government, who were running this place, wanted it to be as homely and hospitable as possible. Mostly because nobody really knew how long they were going to be here. Months. Years. Who knows?

Anything was possible.

Avi heard the clicking noise outside the door. He felt his body shaking as he stepped over to the door to take a look. The clicking wasn't like footsteps or anything like that. It was unusual. Something he wasn't used to.

Animal, almost.

He looked around outside. He could smell a whiff of the breakfasts, which were already beginning their cooking. His stomach churned. He hoped it'd be pizza today. *Please, God, give me pizza.*

He couldn't see anything, so he stepped back.

And then he saw the darkness.

He couldn't explain it any other way. Just a dark shadow, right outside his room.

He narrowed his eyes and tried to focus on it. But the more he tried to focus, the more this shadow's form changed to something less than solid.

He could hear the clicking noise very loudly now. He knew for a fact it was coming from that shadow.

He took a step back. He had an alarm by the side of his bed, as did everyone.

One click of it, and the security teams would be alerted right away.

He took another step back.

The shadow stayed completely still.

He looked away from it, just for a second, to get an idea where the security button was.

When he looked back, the shadow was right in front of him.

He scrambled for the security button.

He was already too late.

The shadow swallowed him up.

One second, there was a minuscule scream, that only four people in this entire complex would hear, before rolling over and returning to their sleep.

The next second, Avi was...

[35]

I watched the mass of crafts surround me and the rest of the Resistance and I knew now was the time we stood up and fought—for the good of ourselves, and for the good of everyone.

The sky was completely black, not only because of the sheer size of the mothership, but also the wall of crafts right in front of us.

Everywhere I looked, left to right, right to left, those crafts were all there in lines, watching and waiting.

I heard the silent hum coming from them, as they waited, and we waited. I sensed what this stand-off was. One final opportunity for us to turn around and to give up.

And in a way, knowing that was on the table reassured me and motivated me going forward. Because I knew that it meant the mothership and Alternate Kyle were pulling out all the stops to make sure we didn't get anywhere near the inside of that ship.

They'd brought out the heavy artillery to deal with us. I took that as a compliment.

"Are you sure about this?"

I looked to my right.

It was Damon. His throat was wobbling, and I could see his eyes were wide, like they always were whenever he was afraid.

I put my hand on his shoulder. "Hey," I said. "We're tough. We've got this. Right, man?"

Damon looked at me then and smiled. "You're tough. Way tougher than me. Never thought I'd say that, but it's true."

I felt flattered to hear Damon say those words. Growing up, he'd always been my rock. I always looked to him when things weren't going so well. He had a way of making everything seem irrational, or irrelevant. He'd tell me to take my problem and picture the worst case scenario. The absolute worst. When I'd done that, I often realized my worries weren't as strong, especially when I started rolling those worries back and planning for the worst.

He had a way of calming me. I was both scared and delighted to have him by my side. I wasn't sure what I'd do without him.

"It's not true," I said. "We're all here because we're all as strong as each other. And that's what we have to believe. Right now."

I moved away from Damon and looked back up at the army of crafts, all standing in our way.

"Any chance you can do your party trick about now?" Roadrunner asked.

I knew what she was referring to. The *feeling* that I got in touch with, deep inside my body.

"I can try," I said.

But I didn't.

I couldn't.

The crafts all flew toward me and the rest of the Resistance. They flew faster than I'd ever seen them fly before. Their tentacles reached out in front of them and solidified, opening up and firing blasts of those energy balls at us at a rapid pace.

Fear paved way for acceptance. I lifted my hands and formed a shield of ice, right above us. "Push back!" I shouted.

The energy balls smacked into the shield of ice. I could see it cracking in places, and I knew it wasn't going to last forever.

But I couldn't feel that tingling sensation.

I wasn't in touch with it yet.

But hell. Did I need to be?

"It's gonna break," Orion shouted. "Glacies. It's going to..."

He didn't finish.

The shield of ice broke.

The crafts poured through.

My stomach sank. I knew then that there was no mere defending ourselves from the crafts. And I knew that the rest of the Resistance would understand that, too.

The time for defense was over.

This was our attack. Not theirs.

I turned over my arms and sent two long blades of ice stretching from my palms.

I flew into the first of the crafts

It swung its tentacles at me, trying to knock me from the sky like so many of its fellow workers already had.

I dodged out of the way of the tentacles, then swung the ice sword down against the metal.

The craft stopped, just for a few seconds, like it didn't quite understand what had just happened.

"Yeah," I said. "Too right."

Then I brought both of the blades together and tore the craft in two.

That wasn't the only one, though, of course. There were at least a thousand more of them following on.

With each of them, I followed the same calm, methodical process. Sliced the tentacle, then sliced the craft. Tentacle, craft, tentacle, craft. The more I took down, the more my confidence grew. This wasn't going to be easy. It wasn't going to be over anytime soon. But we were going to win. We were going to get inside the mothership, rescue Vortex, and take down Alternate Kyle in the process.

I looked around. The rest of the Resistance were fighting off crafts of their own. Roadrunner was bouncing around them and disorienting them. Damon and Cassie were frazzling their circuitry with their electricity. Stone was thumping them harder and harder, the need to locate Vortex driving his painful fight back.

Orion, Saint, and Daniel stood together, using their collective strength in different ways to take down as many as they could.

I felt proud, for a second. Proud not just of them, but of myself.

I was strong enough after all.

I was stronger than I'd ever believed.

I was—

Something wrapped around my wrists and snapped the icy swords from my palms.

I spun around.

There was a massive craft holding on to me. It was far bigger than any others I'd seen. So big that I couldn't even see behind it.

Its tentacles started reeling me in toward its gaping metal mouth.

I struggled to break free. I tried to fire ice, but I was losing my grip. I looked back, saw Cassie looking at me, fear on her face.

Then more crafts swarmed around her, and Damon, and

before we knew it, all of us were captives to these larger crafts, all being reeled in...

And then I felt the tingling sensation.

It was more instant this time. I got a grip of it quicker than I had before.

As I hurtled toward the craft, I let out a roar.

And then a burst of light shot out of my chest.

My neck jolted back so hard that I heard it crack. My arms and legs fired backward, too.

I felt the energy pouring out of my body. I couldn't see anything, just stars in the sky. I thought they looked beautiful.

While I wasn't totally sure of what was happening, I didn't resist the energy leaving me. I didn't try to control it. That was part of my problem altogether. I tried to control my thoughts and my actions too much.

Right now, I knew that thoughtlessness was surely working in my favor.

A few seconds—or maybe minutes—later, I came back to the present.

The first thing I noticed was the silence.

There was a total silence to the air. I truly believed right then the stories I'd heard that there was no sound in space, at least not by the definition we knew it. I floated around and looked at what had happened.

Clouds of dust floated before me.

The clouds of dust where the crafts had once hovered.

All of them, gone.

I looked back.

The Resistance were all still floating, too. All in awe.

Our path to the mothership was free.

This was our opportunity.

"Come on," I said. "Now's the time we—"

"No," a voice said.

It was so cold, so sharp, that it made my skin crawl.

The worst part about it, though?

I recognized it.

I recognized it very well.

I looked back up at the mothership.

Alternate Kyle was hovering in front of its entrance. He was wearing all black, with a hood pulled over his head. He was looking right down at me. Me in particular.

"Now's the time your little journey ends," he said.

[36]

"What? You look surprised to see me. Like this isn't my mothership you're hovering in front of."

I swallowed the lump in my throat as I stared up at Alternate Kyle. Despite the difference in his attire, I could definitely tell that he was a future version of myself. The same build. The same little dimple on the bottom of his chin, which I hadn't up to this point even known I had. And that same twang to his voice.

And yet, as much as I knew this man was a version of myself—and as sure as I was that the rest of the Resistance would be understanding that now, too—there was nothing I had in common with this *version* of myself, if I could call it that.

"Anyway," Alternate Kyle said. "I don't know why we're hanging around outside. The edge of the Earth's atmosphere is a cold place. You should come inside. See my home."

I clenched my hands together and readied myself to attack, knowing damn well that this was my chance to defeat him and get Vortex back.

But in the space of a second, I blinked, and when I opened my eyes, I was inside.

"Welcome to my home. This is probably my favorite room of them all."

I was struck right away by the sheer size of this room. It was unlike anything I'd ever seen. The ceilings went higher than the eye could see, and it stretched on so far that I couldn't even see the other end. Although Alternate Kyle had brought us in here because it was cold outside, a shiver crept up my arms, and I felt far colder in here than I had out there.

Alternate Kyle stretched out his arms. He was standing a few meters in front of me. "Well? What do you think?"

I took a deep breath and made a solid pair of icy gloves wrap around my fists. "Vortex. Where is she?"

Alternate Kyle tilted his head to the right. "I thought you'd ask that. You don't have to worry, though. She's okay. Really."

Stone started running toward Alternate Kyle. "You bastard. If you've laid a finger on her, I'll kill you. I'll—"

Alternate Kyle lifted a hand.

Stone flew right up into the air.

I activated my abilities some more. I heard Cassie and Damon's electricity spark, and Roadrunner started to run in Stone's direction. All of us were primed for attack.

"I wouldn't," Alternate Kyle said. "Not if you ever want to see any of your friends again."

I kept myself positioned ready to attack. But in the end, I looked at Cassie and the others and nodded, signaling them to lower their arms.

As they did, I saw a smile creep up Alternate Kyle's face. "Good. That's more like it. Stone always was stubborn. I know that for a fact, just as you know it now. And you know it's better if we deal with one another without his bravado getting in the way."

None of us said a word.

"Oh come on," he said, lowering his hands to either side. "You're all thinking it, aren't you? I know you are. Hell, I know each of you better than you know yourselves right now."

Adrenaline coursed through my body. In the corners of this deathly dark room, I swore I saw eyes peering at me. "I don't care what you have to say for yourself," I said. "Hand over Vortex. That's what we're here for. That's all we're here for."

"But it's not 'all you're here for' really, is it? Don't take me for naive, Kyle. Remember, I was you once."

"You were never me. We're not the same."

I saw Alternate Kyle's smile even more, then, underneath his hood. "Oh, you're wrong about that. You're so, so wrong."

He started to walk toward me. As he did, I felt the hair on my arms stand on end, like he was made up of static.

"Haven't you ever wondered where I came from?"

I watched him walk closer and closer. Of course I'd wondered where he came from. But I couldn't let any of those thoughts or speculations cloud my mind right now.

I had a feeling I was going to find out a lot more very soon anyway.

"I'm from the future, Kyle. Not an alternate dimension. Nothing like that. Just the future."

I felt my throat go dry. "How?"

"The 'how' goes beyond what your present mind has the ability to understand. That goes for all of you. But rest assured, in the future—a long, long time into the future—I gain the abilities to travel back in time. Now, it's not all plain sailing. I can't pick and choose the moment I travel back to. But I found this moment. And I realize this is the perfect moment. It's the way it's supposed to be."

Alternate Kyle was right. It was hard for me to comprehend that time travel had been cracked, however far into the future he was from. But then, I'd seen glimpses of it, hadn't I? I'd watched seconds turn back during the last few days, accompanied by that tingling sensation, as if there was something stronger inside of me that I hadn't quite fully managed to understand or embrace yet.

"I've been in the future. Far, far into the future. And of course, I started off like you. Positive. Optimistic. Arrogant. Afraid. But mostly, naive.

I saw the good times that followed your takedown of Catalyst. Then I saw the co-existence of ULTRAs and people. And for a long time, it works. It really does. But then, I've seen what ULTRAs do to their home. And I can't allow that same destruction to happen. Not again."

My head spun with all this new information. "If you care so much about our home, then why are you destroying it?"

Alternate Kyle smiled and shook his head. "I'm not talking about Earth, Kyle. I'm talking about this entire universe."

I staggered a bit to one side when he said those words. The silence from the rest of the Resistance said it all, too. "The universe?" I said.

"I told you there were things you wouldn't be able to understand. Not truly. But yes. The universe. Humanity and ULTRAs reach a stage where they can expand to new planets and new galaxies. And for a time, it works. But then everything goes wrong. Humanity is destroyed. The entire universe is on the verge of collapse, all because of the power of the ULTRAs. I've seen it, and I know it happens. So now I have to make sure the ULTRAs don't go anywhere for the sake of the universe and every life form in it."

"This is mad. This is... this is insane."

"I have to alter history, Kyle. For the people I love, who are the people you love. I've been capturing ULTRAs so I can use their energy to create something... well, something that will do the job. After that, there will be no more pain and no more suffering. Just know that... that all our friends here and elsewhere go on to have good, happy, long lives. And you... *we* make the ultimate sacrifice, right here, for the preservation of life. Isn't that a sacrifice worth making?"

I looked at Orion, Saint, Daniel. I looked at Cassie, Roadrunner, Damon. Up above, I could see a light silhouette where Stone was. I wanted to believe it was a necessary sacrifice. That Alternate Kyle was genuinely looking out for the world's best interests.

"I can't," I said.

Alternate Kyle narrowed his eyes. "You what?"

"I can't accept destruction because I don't believe that the future you are talking about is inevitable. I can't just let you kill my friends."

Alternate Kyle sighed, then. He genuinely looked disappointed. "Very well. I hoped I wouldn't have to do this. But..."

In the blink of an eye, one moment, there was nobody beside Alternate Kyle.

The next, Vortex and...

"Avi?"

Avi was battered and bruised, perched on his knees. He looked out of it.

Vortex didn't look much better. I didn't think I'd ever seen her so worn down.

I took a step forward, but right away I felt weaker, somehow, like I was drowning in thick layer after layer of tar.

I tried to spark up my abilities, but I couldn't.

I wasn't strong enough.

I was just Kyle Peters again. Not Glacies, but Kyle Peters.

Alternate Kyle stretched out his hands, one to Vortex's head, and one to Avi's head.

"I'm sorry, Kyle. I'm sorry."

I saw the ice brighten up in Alternate Kyle's palms.

I saw it creep from his hands and charge up, right beside Avi and Vortex's heads.

"No."

I wanted to fight. I wanted to. And for a moment, I thought that voice I'd heard saying no, resisting, was my own.

And then I saw Damon lunging forward, right at Alternate Kyle.

"Damon!" I shouted.

He looked back at me as he flew toward Alternate Kyle. And just for a moment, as his arms sparked with electricity, I saw a smile on his face.

"You were right, man," he said. "I am stronger than I thought."

And then he flew into Alternate Kyle, and what happened next would never leave me, not for the rest of my life.

Alternate Kyle turned his hands away from Vortex and Avi.

He pointed them at Damon.

"Damon!" I screamed.

I lunged forward after them, but it felt like I was running in clay.

"Damon, no!"

Then, I heard a blast.

A blast that split through the entire mothership.

I heard shouting around me. I heard cries. I knew things were going on. Conflict. Fighting. Battle. Vaguely, somewhere beside me, I heard Daniel telling me we were getting the hell out of here.

But I couldn't do a thing.

I couldn't act.

All I could do was stare at Damon's crippled body as he lay there on the metal.

All I could do was watch as my best friend—the friend I'd

grown up with, the friend who'd stood by my side through high school, the friend who'd hooked me up with Ellicia in the first place—breathed his last breaths.

"We'll... we'll go to the next Ethan Hunt movie," Damon muttered.

Tears rolled down my face as explosions cracked above me, flashing either side of me. "No, Damon. Please. Please."

He grabbed my hand with his shaky grip. "It's okay," he said. "You are strong. You are s..."

And then, my best friend closed his eyes.

He didn't open them again.

[37]

Two weeks later

I WALKED along Damon's street and prepared to deliver the horrifying news that I was still struggling to accept myself.

It was morning, and a bright one at that. There was a cool breeze, which blew discarded Coca-Cola bottles and takeout packs across the street. But really, everything just looked so beautiful this morning.

It was a shame about the circumstances.

The mothership had gone. The crafts had retreated. Christmas had passed by without any real hoo-rah. It was strange, really. After all, I'd faced off with Alternate Kyle and he'd told me that his job was to make sure no UTLRAs made it with their abilities. I still had my abilities. And the other survivors of that horrible day two weeks ago—all of them, thankfully—still had their abilities. Vortex aside.

Vortex was in hospital. She had been there for a couple of

weeks now. She was weak, and Stone visited her every day. She was powerless. But she was alive. That was the main thing.

There was one who hadn't survived, though. Just thinking about him made my knees go weak and sickness creep up into my throat at the thought of never seeing him again, never laughing and joking and enjoying his company.

Damon.

Damon had made the ultimate sacrifice to save Vortex and Avi's lives.

Damon was gone.

And now that we knew for certain, now we'd mustered up the courage, it was time to tell his family the truth.

Avi walked on my left side and Ellicia on my right. Ellicia had been released from the safe zone in Montana just three days ago. The government had decided that for whatever reason, the mothership had stopped its assault on Earth.

I knew that wasn't true. I knew, deep down, that it'd be back. I'd seen the look in Alternate Kyle's eyes, and I knew that look because it was my own look.

A look of focus. A look of total determination.

I still hadn't accepted that Damon was gone. After all, it was hard to. Cassie was back. Orion and Daniel had come back. Even *I* had come back. Up to now, the only person I'd lost that was close to me was Mom, and sometimes I wondered if there were a chance she'd come back someday, too.

But Damon...

I'd seen what'd happened to him, what Alternate Kyle had done to him.

I knew there was no coming back from that.

At least it would've been quick.

We reached Damon's house. I stood at the end of the pathway leading up to it.

Ellicia squeezed my hand. "You sure you want to do this?"

My throat wobbled. I had to fight to hold back the tears. "No," I said. "But I have to. It has to be me."

She half-smiled at me, then kissed me. I could taste the tears on her lips.

Then, Avi patted me on my back.

"Good luck, bruv," he said. "You go do what you have to do."

I hugged him, tightly. I knew Avi and I were going to have to stick together, real close, after what'd happened to Damon. It felt like the life and soul of our group had been torn away, and that nothing would ever be the same between us again.

I cleared my throat, adjusted my collar.

Then I walked up the pathway toward Damon's front door.

When I reached it, lifted my hand, I stopped for a second. Everything in my mind told me I couldn't do this. That there had to be another way. Because saying it out loud was accepting it was the truth, and I didn't want to believe it was the truth.

In the end, I didn't even have to open the door.

Damon's mom, Sally, opened it before I'd even knocked.

Sally was a short, thin woman with light gray hair. She looked older than she actually was. She frowned when she saw me, then Avi and Ellicia behind me. "Kyle?" she said. "What're you..." she must've been baffled that I was still even alive. "What's..."

Then it happened. It clicked. I saw it, the grief and the realization and everything hitting her right in that instant, tearing her life apart.

"I'm sorry, Sally. I'm so sorry."

"No," she said, shaking her head, tears starting to roll down her face. "No."

"He was brave. But he's gone."

"No."

"Damon's gone."

"No!"

I saw her cover her face with her hands. She dropped down to her knees and let out a grieving moan, which didn't even sound human. Tears rolled down my cheeks now, too.

I moved down toward her. "I'm so sorry. I'm—"

"Get away," she snapped.

I jolted back.

Sally looked... not just grief-stricken, but furious.

Actually furious, at me.

"Sally, I—"

"You did this!" she shouted, pointing a wobbling finger at me. "He was my boy and you—you got him involved with those ULTRAs. You did this!"

As I stood there on my best friend's pathway watching his grieving mother blame me for his death, I felt a lot of things.

But mostly, I felt like I needed to run.

"I am sorry," I said, turning away and rushing down the pathway. "I really, really am."

Ellicia reached out for me when I got to the end of the pathway. "Kyle. It'll take time. She just needs—"

But I didn't stick around to hear what she had to say.

I pretended to teleport myself somewhere far, far away.

Instead, I just made myself invisible and ran as fast as I could up the street.

No matter how far I ran, tears blotting out my vision, I couldn't escape Sally's wails of grief, and I couldn't get her words out of my head.

You did this!

[38]

Hielo looked down at Damon's broken body, and he felt a tear roll down his cheek.

Although it had been many, many years since he knew Damon, and he had known many people since—fought many battles, made allies, lost them to betrayal, made new ones —nothing compared to Damon.

Damon was his *friend.*

And he'd killed him.

He crouched down and covered Damon's body with a blanket. His throat wobbled as all the memories of the good times he'd had with Damon, back when he'd been just a child, filled his memories joyously. He found himself smiling as he recalled the time Damon forgot to bring his shorts for football practice and decided to play wearing his pants. He found himself grimacing at the time they'd had that nasty argument because Kyle thought Damon had stolen one of his Pokemon cards—a crime which, of course, Damon hadn't committed.

He looked down at Damon and he felt truly, truly sorry for the way this had ended.

"I'm sorry," he muttered. "But you had a good life, in my

reality. You lived until you were three-hundred and forty. And you never ever fell out with me. Never again."

He clicked his fingers, and Damon's body disappeared.

"Goodbye, old friend."

"Hielo?"

Hielo flinched when he heard the voice. He turned around and saw B3484 standing there, looking somewhat concerned about his attachment to the people that were supposed to be enemies. "Sorry. I just needed some time."

B3484 shuffled over to Hielo's side. "That's quite alright, sir. I just wanted to let you know that we're all charged and ready to execute the plan."

The plan. Just the thought of it made Hielo's skin crawl. "You've absorbed enough ULTRA energy to be positive you can lift every human from the face of the earth and toward the Andromeda galaxy? For their own protection? You're absolutely sure?"

"Of course, you and I know we can't speak in absolutes—"

"But you're as sure as you can be?"

"I believe I am, yes."

Hielo looked at the spot where Damon had fallen.

Then he stood up and walked over to his enormous glass window, which looked out over Earth.

"Then commence the plan," he said. "Get every human off Earth. Then destroy Earth and every ULTRA on it."

"Are you sure this is what you want to do, sir?"

Hielo's heart raced. "It's the only way we can guarantee the safety of the universe. Otherwise, history will repeat itself. We can't allow that to happen."

"But you do realize that once we've triggered the energy, there will be—"

"Zero chance of us surviving. Yes. I understand that."

A pause from B3484. "And you're still sure you want to proceed?"

He felt for B3484. It was like this artificial intelligence was facing up to its own mortality for the very first time. "I'm positive," he said. "Save the humans. Destroy Earth. Begin the preparations. Now."

He thought about Damon.

He knew he was doing the right thing.

[39]

I hovered over the mouth of the Hekla volcano, and it felt like I was right back at the beginning again.

The sun was setting. It was so peaceful here in Iceland, and it always would be. There wasn't any humanity around for miles. I could keep a low profile and just hover over the mouth of this volcano for as long as I wanted.

And that suited me fine.

I just wanted to keep a low profile, now.

I just wanted to disappear into obscurity.

I listened to the breeze beneath me, so peaceful as it blew against the sides of the volcano. If I closed my burning eyes, I could see myself far away from here, on a beach, Mom and Dad by my side, Cassie splashing in the water, and Ellicia, Avi, and Damon all with me, having a laugh.

Every thought of Damon made my mind and body turn to jelly.

I wasn't ever going to forgive myself for what had happened to him.

I opened my eyes and looked down into the lava. It spat up

toward me. I sensed the anger of the world in my direction, all of it bubbling up and getting ready to explode.

But mostly, I saw myself. I saw the reason I'd failed, and what my problem had been all along.

I didn't believe in myself. I didn't see myself as strong enough. That was the issue.

Sure, I'd hidden behind my Glacies persona. And for so many years, that persona had given me strength.

But regardless of how much I tried to convince myself otherwise, the Glacies persona wasn't strong enough. I might have abilities. Hell, I might *physically* be the most powerful ULTRA to have lived.

But underneath all of that, I was still Kyle Peters.

It was Kyle Peters who was haunted by his regrets.

It was Kyle Peters who was crippled by self-doubt.

It was Kyle Peters who had failed, time after time, again and again.

I moved closer to the mouth of the volcano. I felt the heat cover me like a warm blanket rapidly turning nasty. I kept on going, though, even as I started to cough. Part of me wondered what it'd be like if I just threw myself down there, into the flames. Who would notice? Who would care, really? Sure, my dad would be sad. Avi and Ellicia would miss me. But time would go on, and I'd soon be forgotten. Most of the world thought I was dead anyway, and they seemed to be getting on just fine without me.

After all, it was me who had come back in future form to sort the old problems that the world had.

It was my future self who blamed me and all of ULTRA-kind for a future of violence and terror.

Maybe it would be better for everyone if I didn't stick around much longer.

I pushed myself further into the heat, the skin on my face starting to fry.

Then I sighed, and I hovered back to the mouth of the volcano.

I couldn't do a thing like that. I didn't even have the strength or the courage to do that.

I had to be strong enough as Kyle. I had to *be* Kyle because Kyle was Glacies, and I had to make Kyle the strongest person he could be.

Even if I couldn't, I had to try.

But...

What did I have to try for anymore?

Damon was gone. I was already too late.

What good was trying to be someone else now the time for action had passed?

I pulled my Glacies gear out in front of me, then. I felt my bottom lip shaking and watched a tear drop down from my eyes and onto the gear. I remembered the pride I'd felt when I'd first put this gear on. How much stronger it made me feel.

But really, it was all just an illusion.

It didn't make me stronger at all.

It just clouded my judgment for a while.

I held out the outfit in front of me, and I saw the lava spit up once again, as the egg-smelling sulfur drowned my senses.

I had nothing left to fight for.

There was nothing left for me to do anymore, as Glacies.

I was done now.

"Goodbye," I whispered.

Then I dropped the Glacies gear down into the volcano.

I watched as it fell into it. For a moment, I wanted to go down there and stop it falling. I felt weak—naked, even —without it.

But then it hit the lava and it disappeared in the space of a second.

I wasn't Glacies anymore.

I was just Kyle Peters.

[40]

"So. It's taken a while. But here we are, on Earth, grabbing a beer. Who'd have thought it, hmm?"

Orion cracked open a beer and sipped back the fizzy liquid inside. It was non-alcoholic beer, of course. He didn't like alcohol. It severely affected his judgment.

Saint, however, had a *real* can of beer, of which he had already sipped down half. He looked at Orion like he was stupid, on his fake beer.

"What?" Orion asked.

Saint frowned. "Just... zero alcohol? In times like these? Really?"

Orion sipped some of it. Truth be told, he wasn't even liking this fake stuff. "I don't like real beer."

"Nonsense. Nobody dislikes real beer."

"Well, you've finally met someone who does."

Saint tilted his head to one side and sipped that beer back, finishing it off. He crinkled up the can, crushing it in his palms, threw it into the distance, then grabbed another one.

"Shouldn't you go slower on those?" Orion asked.

Saint stopped for a second. He had his mask off, which

revealed the true extent of his scarred face. "I'm not going slower. Especially not during a special occasion like this. And neither should you."

He telekinetically made a can of beer appear right in front of Orion.

"So are you going to drink, or not?"

Orion felt the bubbles popping on the edge of his tongue.

Then he sighed and took the beer.

"I guess I don't have a choice," he said.

"No. You don't."

Orion cracked open the beer, and together with Saint, he drank as they sat there in the middle of the Sahara desert.

"I used to come here," Saint said. "When I needed a little... downtime."

"Downtime from attempting to destroy the world? Never have guessed you might've needed it."

Saint smirked, and drank some more beer. "You know, as hard as it must be for you to believe this, I never hated you."

"Yes. It is hard to believe."

"I never detested you. If anything, I respected you. You stood up for your values and fought for what you believe in, just like I do. I can't help admiring you for that."

Orion shook his head. "You and I aren't like one another. Make no mistake about that."

"There is something you do have to thank me for, of course."

"Go on. What's that?"

"Kyle. Cassie. They wouldn't have the strength they had if it weren't for me."

The beer turned to a bitter taste in Orion's mouth. He remembered the past, as ugly as it was. The battle with Saint. And even before that, taking his two children to Saint in order to cure them, only to find them turned into ULTRAs instead. Then them being taken away from him and forced to live a life where he wasn't their father at all. "Don't you dare take credit for the pain you've caused my family."

"Pain? Sure. But without Kyle, the world wouldn't even be here anymore. You could say, in a sense, that I was the architect of my own downfall."

"I'd say you're an arrogant asshole who needs reminding that he isn't the good guy. You're just not the biggest bad guy in this situation."

"And who is? Your son, who flies up there however old he is, promising to purge the world of all its badness?"

Orion couldn't help taking on board what Saint was saying —as hard as that was to admit. If the man in the mothership really was a future version of his son, then didn't that change everything he thought he knew?

"Face it," Saint said, finishing off another beer. "There are no good people and there are no bad people. There are just morals, which are individual things anyway, and there is perspective. To future Kyle, what he's doing must seem right. He wouldn't be trying to eliminate the people he cares about so dearly if it wasn't."

"And I'll bet you're loving this all, aren't you?" Orion asked.

Saint shrugged. "I've dabbled with humanity's imprisonment. ULTRAs, well, they long ago proved their problematic nature to me. I'd be lying if I said part of this isn't satisfying."

Orion clenched his fist. One wrong word, and he'd put Saint down.

"But," Saint said, continuing, as he opened another beer. "I am able to look back and reflect. And I do see that, in my darker moments, I made some mistakes."

He didn't continue that statement. He just left it at that. And when Orion saw how sincerely Saint was looking at him, he realized that was the closest he was ever going to get to an apology.

Orion wanted to say something back to Saint. He wanted to open up some more. He couldn't lie—he was enjoying sharing a moment with his oldest ULTRA associate, foe as he may have been.

But he didn't get to finish his conversation.

The sky lit up with green light.

He looked up. Saint lowered his head.

The light shot through the clouds. Around it, the clouds parted, then started to move upwards as if they were being dragged from the Earth's atmosphere.

"What is this?" Orion asked.

Saint sipped back some more of his beer. "This is the end," he said. "Unless..."

Saint didn't have to finish.

They both knew what the "unless" was about.

They both knew *who* the "unless" was about.

The fate of the world depended on Kyle Peters, aged nineteen.

If he didn't pull himself together, the world would fall.

He was Earth's last hope.

"To Glacies," Saint said, lifting his can of beer into the air and gesturing it toward Orion.

Orion hesitated, as he felt a strong breeze sucking him to that opening and saw stormier conditions gradually growing down on earth—wind, rain, lightning.

Then, he lifted his can and tapped it against Saint's. "To Kyle."

Together, they sat back and drank, as the contents of the Earth started to float up into the sky.

Together, they waited, in hope that the last hero would prevent the fall, once again.

[41]

It was when I sat on the edge of the rock in the middle of the Australian outback that my life changed again.

The sun was setting, casting a beautiful orange glow over the horizon. It was the Australian summer, so it was staggeringly scorching. I knew I could cool myself down with my ice if I needed to, but honestly, I didn't really want to.

I had teleported my way here, sure. And, of course, sometimes I'd have to use my powers in stickier situations.

But I wasn't just going to use them for no real reason anymore.

Glacies had run his course.

There was nothing else I could do.

I sipped back some cola, the taste of it stinging my mouth. I'd been under for so long that I'd forgotten just how refreshing the drink was, but also how sugary it was.

It didn't stop me drinking it, though. Like taking candy from a baby.

I listened to the sound of the wind brushing past me, and smelled the earthiness of the scorched ground. I'd failed

Damon. And by extension, I'd failed, full-stop. Sure, I might be moping, but what else was there for me to do now? What other purpose did I serve? What other role did I have to fulfill?

I was about to crack open another cola when I heard a whooshing noise.

When I looked around, I saw Daniel Peters—Nycto—walking over toward me.

"Oh, hey," I said. "Good of you to join me. I was just opening another cola."

Daniel snatched the cola from my hand with his mind and made the can burst all over me.

"Hey," I said. "You can pay for that."

He grabbed me by the scruff of the neck then and pushed me down to the earth.

Instinctively, I punched back. But it was a weak, powerless punch.

"So this is what you are now, is it?" he spat, the disdain clear to hear in his voice. "You're just a quitter?"

"I didn't quit."

"Yes, you did," he said, pushing me down harder. "You didn't get your way, so you've given up. You've spat your dummy out."

I pushed back harder this time, using some of my abilities in the process. "And what else am I supposed to do? Keep fighting and watch more people die?"

"Damon died," Daniel said, returning my push. "And I'm sorry for that. Really. But you can't just give up on everyone else just because you can't face screwing up again."

I felt my skin crawl. I kicked Daniel between the legs, right into the air. Then I flew up there and grabbed him, me with the ascendancy and the elevation on him now. "Don't talk about Damon like I could've stopped what happened."

"Why?" Daniel spat. "You blame yourself for his death. And you know, maybe you're right to."

I wrapped my hands around Daniel's stomach and went pounding to the ground.

He vanished, just as I hit the solid earth, and left me with a mouthful of blood and sand.

I turned onto my back, cracking my bones back into place. Daniel was standing over me, in a cloud of dust. "Kyle, I'm not doing this because I want to punish you or anything like that."

"Then what do you want?"

"I'm doing it because you are strong. And there's so much left to fight for."

Deep down, I knew Daniel was right. I lowered my head, unable to face up to the shame I felt for giving up on everyone, all because I didn't believe I was powerful enough anymore. "Alternate Kyle's from the future. There's no point fighting the inevitable."

Daniel smirked at that and shook his head.

"What?"

"Nothing."

"No, what? What's so funny?"

"Look, I'm not a time travel expert, but something tells me you *aren't* supposed to die at all. Because there you are, still living, in the future."

I narrowed my eyes. "Right. You've really lost me now."

"Bear with me," Daniel said, crouching opposite me. "You are still alive many, many years into the future. And I dunno. Maybe something does go wrong. Maybe what future you is doing does turn out justified, all along."

"You're saying I should just let the world burn?"

Daniel shook his head. "Quite the opposite. I'm saying you should fight. You should stand up to Alternate Kyle. Because sure, things might go shitty a zillion years in the future. But right now, and going forward, we need you. The world needs you."

The future stuff was giving me a headache. But I could see Daniel's point. "I just don't know what I'm supposed to do."

Daniel tilted his head to one side.

Then he put a hand on my shoulder and immediately teleported the pair of us out of the outback.

"You could start with this," he said.

In front of me, there was a massive light beaming down into Earth's surface. Around it, a whirlpool-like phenomenon sucked everything up toward it. Mostly people. The ground shook with its intensity.

My heart pounded. I could barely speak. "What... what is..."

"I don't know what it is," Daniel said. "Not yet. But I can't see it being a good thing. Can you?"

I watched as the green light powered down against the earth's crust. Part of me already knew what this was. "ULTRA energy," I said.

"Huh?"

"This is what he was taking the ULTRA energy for. Using it to create something to... to take humans off the face of the earth. To protect them. And then..."

I stopped then, because it all clicked.

"Oh, God," I said.

"What is it?"

My mind spiraled as the truth dawned. "He's going to destroy Earth. He's going to leave ULTRAs here and wipe us out."

I took a few steps toward the light. As afraid as I was, as terrified as I was, and as exposed without my Glacies gear as I was, I knew there was no giving up now. I had to fight.

"Does that mean the fight's back on?" Daniel asked. He held out a hand.

I studied it for a few seconds as the ground beneath me shook.

Then, I took it.

"Let's go get a team together," I said.

[42]

Orion. Saint. Cassie. Daniel. Stone. Roadrunner.

I stood opposite all of them above the city, the green light dragging the contents of the Earth up and away, and I said the words that I knew would be some of the most important I ever spoke.

"What we're about to do is going to be tough. Impossible, perhaps."

Stone nodded. "If it avenges the bastards who wrecked Vortex's abilities then I'm all in for whatever."

I half-smiled sympathetically in return. "There's no guarantee any of us will come back from this alive."

Roadrunner puffed out her lips. "I'm kind of tired of living, anyway. With all these responsibilities, it's getting a little overrated."

"But you have to trust me when I tell you that we are stronger together. And when we are together, we can take down anyone, and anything."

I saw the uncertainty on Cassie's face.

"You can believe in me, sis. I'm done with being Glacies,

sure. But I'm not done with being Kyle Peters. And Kyle Peters is going to fight. For humanity. For ULTRAs. For the planet."

She sighed, then. And a few seconds later, she stepped forward. "I'm in. 100%."

Daniel joined me first. Then Orion soon followed and put a hand on my shoulder. "I'd never abandon your side."

Then it was just Saint left, of all ULTRAs.

"We could use your help," I said. "You're a strong fighter."

Saint smiled then, as if I'd just paid him the highest compliment I possibly could. "Indeed I am."

He stepped forward and together we stood in a circle.

We looked over at another of the green lights as it had smashed into the surface of the earth. We watched the spiraling clouds rapidly rotate, slowly but surely swallowing up the water from the sea, then the vehicles, and then eventually humans themselves.

"Earth might have fallen once," I said. "But not again. Are you ready?"

Everyone looked at one another. They nodded. There was hesitation, of course, but that was to be expected. This was a journey into the abyss. This was a march into the depths of hell.

"For Damon," I said.

"For Damon," everyone repeated.

Then we shot up, following that green bolt of energy, and readied ourselves for war.

[43]

Hielo looked down at the eight green beams as they headed down toward the surface of the Earth, and he waited for the final two to strike.

He knew what would happen when the final two struck. And he felt guilty about it, in a way. Because as long ago as it was that he'd moved away from Earth, as far in the past as that was, that attachment was still there, of course. It was still his world. It was still the place he was born, the place he'd grown up, the place he'd made his first friends and his first enemies, the place he'd thought he was so weak, then discovered he was so, so strong.

In a sense, as he stared out of his wide, open window and down at the Earth as the beams dragged up humanity to somewhere much, much safer—a process that admittedly would take a lot longer than he liked—it was like he was looking back at old videotapes from his youth. Watching the happy memories, so present but at the same time, so different, like he was looking back at something that hadn't even happened at all.

He felt his throat welling up when he thought again of Damon and the loss he'd felt when he'd watched him go. He felt wracked with guilt, having to do what he'd done. But he wouldn't let it cloud his judgment. The future had already happened, and Damon had lived out a long and fulfilling life. Longer and more fulfilling than even he would have ever imagined.

His path had already been carved out ahead of him. His life had already unfolded. So he could have no guilt where that was concerned.

But it *was* difficult.

"Are you ready for the final two beams, sir?"

He heard B9484's—another of his AI friends—voice, and he longed for human—or ULTRA—attachment. He longed for someone else, someone who wasn't artificial, to connect with.

But again, he'd had that life already. He'd lived it. He'd had the friends and he'd had the allies—he'd had it all.

And yet something inside him made him want it all over again. It made him envy Kyle, his past version, because he knew he had that all ahead of him.

That's another reason he had to put a stop to Kyle before he grew any older.

He was destined for an amazing life that would end so bitterly when he realized exactly what his legacy was.

He was doing him a favor, in a sense. Saving him from himself.

But as he stared down at that green beam, a part of him wanted to spare Kyle. To see if he could change him, in any way.

"You should know," B9484 said. "The Resistance, as they call themselves, are on their way here. They seem focused and determined. Would you like us to deal with them?"

Hielo gritted his teeth. Of course the Resistance were heading his way. He had to applaud Kyle's resilience. He admired himself, in a way. His younger self was even stronger than he'd thought.

"The rest of them. Orion. Saint. Daniel. Cassie. (He hesitated when he said their names because he had been so close to all of them in different ways, over the years. But they were a part of the problem, going forward. And he couldn't show any mercy where they were concerned.) Stone. Roadrunner. You can deal with those."

"And Kyle?" B9484 asked. "Because he does appear to be leading the charge. And he is strong. Stronger, perhaps, than we even thought."

Hielo gritted his teeth together and watched the whirlwind spin even faster, dragging all the contents of earth—except the ULTRAs—up into the sky, toward a better future; a paradise.

"Leave Kyle to me," Hielo said. "I want to finish him myself."

[44]

We soared up in the direction of the mothership for one final assault.

An assault that we knew may well be our final ever stand.

Once again, that strange sensation of the daylight vanishing the more we proceeded toward the mothership occurred, and this time it felt suffocating, enough to make even the most headstrong person feel paranoid and claustrophobic. In honesty, I felt bad. Bad that I'd not had the chance to say a proper goodbye to Ellicia, or to Avi, or to Dad. But in all truth, I knew what I was doing was way too important to delay any further.

The air got icier the closer we got to the mothership, further increasing the unease I felt—and that we all felt—about our situation. We kept the green beam of light in our eye line at all times. We wanted to follow it, directly if we had to.

It made a strange, low humming sound, and I knew what that sound was now. It's the sound I heard whenever I was using my abilities, but hadn't even put my finger on up to this point. It must've been what everyone heard when they used their abilities too—the sound of the ULTRA life-force, so much of it drained from the remaining ULTRAs on Earth already.

The rest of us lucky ULTRAs, who'd resisted and survived this far?

They were the ones who were being primed for destruction.

"Here we go," Stone said, when we were just feet away from the mothership. "Close enough to attack?"

I tensed my fists and felt ice stretch up the length of my arms. Up ahead, the mothership, in all its glory. Only there was something different about it now. It seemed to have changed shape, where those eight beams were pummeling out of it. Like it wasn't going to stay floating for much longer when those beams had done their job.

"Close enough to—"

"Watch out!"

I heard Daniel's voice, but by that point, it was already too late.

Another green beam fired out of the bottom of the mothership, right above us.

My body turned cold—and not in the good, icy way that I'd used to my advantage so many times over recent years. I froze—again, not in a good way. I wasn't Glacies. I wasn't strong enough to stop this green beam of light. I wasn't...

I heard the words spinning around my mind as that beam of energy fired down toward me, and I saw what my problem had been, all along.

No belief in myself.

No belief in me, Kyle Peters.

That was the problem.

That was exactly the problem.

So I did something different.

In the space of a millisecond, I created a shield around all of us.

Then I brought us all together.

But the beam was still heading down in our direction. It was getting closer.

And then, as if it was no effort at all, I jolted us away from the beam.

I didn't know if it'd worked for a second. Then I figured the fact that I was contemplating whether it'd worked or not must mean that it had.

"How did you..." Saint started.

Then he stopped.

I wasn't sure if it was because it hurt his pride in some way, affecting his claim to being the world's "most powerful ULTRA," or whether he was just genuinely starting to believe in me.

I couldn't know.

I didn't have time to.

Because from the green beams of electricity, small metal crafts started spewing out.

"This is it!" I shouted.

I fired a blast of ice at the first of the crafts. Then I dodged the next one, disorienting it before opening up a wormhole to send it crashing into the front of the next one.

I kept on moving, fluidly, taking down craft after craft, not thinking about what I was doing at all, just trusting my intuition.

As we fought, I saw the light of the green beam fading somewhat. And as it did, all of us went tumbling back down in the direction of Earth.

I pulled myself back straight and re-oriented the rest of the Resistance too, with a click of a finger.

"Hold strong. We've got this."

"Can't you just do your thing?" Stone shouted, as more crafts zoomed down toward our position.

"My thing?"

"You know. Your craft zapping thing... your weird thing. Your... ah shit. It's too late."

Stone was right.

The crafts bombed down into us.

I shot a shield over the lot of us. A strong, hard shield, more solid than I thought I was even capable of making.

I watched the crafts hurtle into it, one by one. I saw their tentacles try to crack through it, but snap upon contact. I saw their circuitry expose as they split into pieces. I saw some of them pull back, then try to slam down onto the shield even harder, eager to break through.

But there was no breaking through.

Not just because I was using my own strength.

But because I was using the strength of the rest of the Resistance, too.

I didn't know how I was doing it; just that it was something to do with that tingling sensation in my body. I could see a blue light coming from Orion, Saint, Daniel, and the others, and morphing into my body as I pushed that shield harder and harder upwards.

"Push back!" I shouted, moving upwards toward the crafts, trying to fight back.

"I can't—"

"You can!" I shouted. "Push back!"

For a split second, it didn't feel like we were going anywhere.

And then we shot upwards, right through the center of the crafts and headed toward the mothership.

I felt invincible, then, as the shield morphed all around us, protecting us from the onslaught of the crafts. I could *feel* their desperation in the air, like this was a situation they weren't used to or prepared for. And that made me feel somewhat triumphant.

I saw the smiles on the faces of the rest of the Resistance as we got nearer and nearer to the mothership. I saw Orion grinning, and Stone smirking, like everyone felt the same pure strength and belief as me.

I even saw Saint looking at me like he'd never looked at me before.

Like he *believed.*

And then something happened.

The shield split.

I saw the crafts pouring inside our shield, filling it up like water in a sinking bottle.

I tried to shoot at them, but that just weakened my side of the shield, too. We started to slow down. The power of the crafts was just too strong.

"Kyle," a voice said.

I didn't recognize it right away. But when I looked around, I saw it was Saint.

The crafts were crowding around the entrance nearest to him. He was managing to hold them back with his own power.

But he was looking at me with a look of remorse. Of regret. Of inevitability.

"You have to keep on going," he said.

I shook my head. "I won't—"

"You have to. You are the only one who can beat yourself. Now go. Go, before I change my mind."

I felt my chest sink as I understood what Saint was saying, and it was such a strange emotion. All these years of fighting him. All these years of seeing him as the lord of all evil.

And now he was doing what he was doing.

"Thank you," I said, my voice shaking. "Thank you."

Saint pushed back harder against the crafts. They were so close to bursting through that the entire shield was at breaking point now. "And thank you."

"For what?"

"For making me r—"

Saint didn't say anything else.

The crafts split through the second layer of the shield.

He lifted his hands, opened up an enormous wormhole in front of himself, which the crafts were all dragged toward.

He cried out as a light burst from his body, and the wormhole moved in toward him.

"Go!" he screamed.

I shot up into the sky, closer to the mothership, away from Saint and his wormhole.

The rest of the Resistance made it.

But as I looked down, I saw the wormhole right across Saint's chest, now.

I saw the crafts flying into it, scrambling to stop themselves being dragged down into the abyss.

And then I saw the light surround Saint as the wormhole slammed shut.

Then...

The wormhole exploded.

I looked at the light from the explosion for a few seconds. All of us stared on, in awe and amazement and bewilderment of what we'd just witnessed.

A hand landed on my back. It was Orion. "Come on," he said. "It's time to keep moving."

I looked at the residue from that explosion. The dust in the sky from the crafts, and the space where the wormhole had been.

And I looked at Saint's head as it floated through space so

peacefully, detached from his body, which had disappeared into oblivion along with Alternate Kyle's crafts.

Saint was gone.

[45]

As we entered the mothership, I couldn't help but keep looking back down at the spot where Saint had disappeared, sacrificing himself for me and the good of the cause.

The crafts had stopped flowing from the mothership and the green beams—for now. I could see something else charging up along the bottom of the mothership, though. Another beam. And by the looks of things, it was the final beam of all.

I didn't want to risk that beam activating. I didn't want to see what it might mean.

I'd seen what the beams—pure ULTRA energy—were capable of anyway. I didn't want to risk allowing that final one to activate.

"Kyle, we have to keep moving."

It was Daniel. I could sense a tinge of sadness and regret to Daniel's voice too. Obviously, I had mixed feelings about Daniel's reaction. I'd believed for so long that Saint was evil, and knowing that he felt bad about his death should've seemed like a betrayal.

But I knew I felt the same way. A glimmer of regret that things couldn't have worked out differently between us.

That Saint had made the ultimate sacrifice.

There was something else that caught my eye, though. The green beams were all coming from an area right in the middle of the mothership. The more I looked, the more I realized that there were gaps in the body of the mothership, and I could see the source. It was far away, but I could get there. I knew I could make it.

"Come on," Cassie said. "We have to keep going, while we still can."

I took a deep breath and pointed up at that source in the middle of the mothership. "Whatever's creating those beams of energy, I think it's right there."

"Which means?" Stone asked.

"Which means that's where I have to go."

I saw their faces turning, then. The confusion kicking in. "Where *we* need to go, you mean?"

I looked around at them. "You've seen what's happening down there on earth. We need ULTRAs down there to defend it, just in case."

Cassie shook her head. "I'm not leaving your side."

"You have to. If you care about Earth at all, you have to."

"And what're you gonna do?" Daniel asked. Even he sounded concerned, now. "What's your plan?"

I looked up at that energy ball right in the middle of the green beams. I could see the tenth—and presumably final—beam charging up, readying to fire.

"I'm going to go up there," I said. "I'm going to stop that final beam from getting anywhere near Earth. And then I'm going to take down Alternate Kyle, once and for all."

Cassie shook her head. She was crying now. "I can't let you leave, little brother. I can't let you just do this."

"You have to."

She turned around.

It was Orion who spoke.

He was looking at me like he'd looked at me when I thought he'd died that day, when Saint sent him into that wormhole. I knew our roles had been reversed, now. But that this time, what was happening had to happen. It was the only way any of us were going to survive.

No. Survival was off the plate now. I'd accepted that much.

But we were going to save Earth.

That was the important thing.

"As long as we're by Kyle's side, we hold him back," Orion said. "We weigh him down with emotion and with responsibility. Sometimes, they are good things. But Kyle needs to do this alone."

Cassie covered her face with her hands. Daniel didn't look best pleased, either.

I floated down to Cassie's side, and I held her.

"I'm going to save the world, sis," I said. "Even if it is the end of me, I'm going to save it. But I need your help with that. Just in case. Okay?"

She looked at me then, from behind tear-covered hands. "You're not coming back, are you? None of us are?"

I smiled and wiped the tears from her cheeks. "Don't say that. Just... just believe. In yourself. In all of us. Because if I hadn't believed in myself—if I hadn't got over my doubt—I wouldn't be here right now. None of us would."

She smiled back at me then, and I felt like I was young again, listening to her advice as we sat together by that swimming pool.

Then I heard a crack, and saw a flash of light.

The tenth green beam flew out from the center of the mothership and powered toward Earth.

My body tensed up. "There's no more time for goodbyes. No more time for anything. You have... you have to get down there."

Stone nodded. He flew up to me and patted my shoulder. "We'll fight for you, kid. As long as you fight for us."

"Always."

Roadrunner followed, hugging me briefly before shooting off. And then Daniel appeared in front of me.

He stretched out a hand. "Goodbye, I guess."

I pulled him toward me and held him tight. "Goodbye, brother. And you do something for me. You get Ellicia. You keep her safe. You promise."

Then it was just Orion and Cassie left.

Neither of them came to me. Instead, they just stayed where they were, looking at me as the rest of the Resistance headed down to battle.

"What?" I asked. "You aren't going to say goodbye at all?"

"I won't say goodbye," Cassie said. "Because I believe I'll see you again, real soon."

She smiled. And before I could go over and hug her, she vanished.

Then it was just Orion and me.

"Aren't you going, too?"

He hesitated. Floated toward me a little, then back.

And then finally he flew to my side.

"I'd never leave my son to fight alone."

"But you said—"

"Don't argue with me. Just... There's no more time. We know what we have to do."

I wanted to argue with Orion, to tell him to get back down to Earth.

Instead, I hugged him; then I held his hand.

Together, we faced the mothership.

Together, we faced the source of those green light beams as they wreaked havoc on the Earth below.

Together, we stared death right in its eyes.

And then we shot up inside the mothership and into the abyss.

[46]

Orion and I flew toward the source in the center of the mothership. But even as we progressed, relatively conflict-free up to now, there was still a feeling like this was big. Like we were a part of something momentous.

But at the same time, it also felt like we were on our final journey, and that however it ended, it wasn't going to end well for everyone.

We flew through the cracks in the center of the mothership and headed toward the huge beam of light in the middle. Since the ten massive bolts of energy had flown down into Earth, the mothership seemed to have taken on a different form completely. It wasn't so much a mothership anymore as a huge cannon of destructive energy.

As I flew past the energy beam—the one dragging the humans and everything else up from Earth—I wondered whether this was Alternate Kyle's plan all along. Teleport the people away from Earth to some other place—a place he knew about. Then, destroy what was left of the planet.

I could empathize with him that it might seem like the

quickest and most convenient way to solve a supposed ULTRA threat.

But this was Earth.

This was my home. *Everyone's* home.

I wasn't just going to stand by and watch it get destroyed.

I was way, way past just standing by, even if it killed me.

Orion flew alongside me. Part of me was relieved to have him by my side. After all, it helped to have company when you were going to battle. But another part of me couldn't help fearing for him.

I'd lost him once. Twice, if you count the time I'd been dragged away from him as a baby. I didn't want to lose him again.

He looked at me, then, and for just a second, I saw a smile.

Then something hit him.

Dread punched me in the gut. I stopped right away, not steadily, but just getting my bearings. I looked down at the spot where he'd been.

I saw then that Orion was in some kind of solid state. His hands were either side of his head. His legs were tied together by some kind of invisible force.

But his eyes were straining toward me.

"Orion," I said. I flew back down to him. I couldn't just leave him here. I had to fight.

As I got closer, I saw that his eyes weren't straining at me at all.

They were straining *behind* me.

My body went cold.

After a few seconds of realization and of dread, I turned around, slowly.

Alternate Kyle was hovering right in front of the huge, blinding ball of energy.

We were still for a second, both of us. It was as if we were hoping by just floating there, we could each avoid the inevitable battle that was to follow.

I waited longer, totally still. In the corner of my eye, I could see the flashes down on Earth, and I didn't want to look at them because I didn't want to accept.

Then I saw Alternate Kyle tense his fists, and ice stretch up his arms.

I did the same in turn.

But it was already too late. Alternate Kyle had fired the first shot in this stand-off, sending a flurry of small, sharp ice daggers down in my direction.

A few of them hit me, slicing at my face. But once I'd steadied myself, I batted them away, sending them into the sides of the mothership before flying up toward Alternate Kyle myself.

He sent more shots of ice down at me, each of them getting thicker and sharper with every shot. One hit from one of those things and it could be enough to take me down for just as long as Alternate Kyle needed to finish me off.

"You'll never win," he shouted. "This is the future for you. This is inevitable. There's no point resisting. Not anymore."

I tensed my jaw. "Only problem is, you don't know how this plays out, do you?"

I saw Alternate Kyle's eyebrows narrow, like he was trying to wrap his head around another facet of time travel—and hell was time travel confusing.

In his moment of confusion, I clapped my hands and opened up a tornado of a whirlpool right beneath him.

Alternate Kyle struggled as the whirlpool of energy sucked him in. He tried to shoot his powers, but he kept on descending into it.

Adrenaline filled my body. My heart pounded. "Is that it? Is that all you've g..."

I stopped when I saw him click his fingers and turn the whirlpool into ice.

Then, the whirlpool smashed apart, and he came flying at me, daggers of light in his palms.

I braced myself and covered myself in a shield. I looked over my shoulder quickly, just to see if Orion was okay.

He was still beneath me. Still in that trapped state. Still—

I felt something hit my right side, and I knew already that it was Alternate Kyle.

I went flying down, back down the way I'd come from. As I hurtled down from such a dizzying height, I saw myself getting closer to Orion. I needed to stay away from him. This wasn't his battle. This was *my* battle. I had to fight for him.

I stuck out my arms and, telekinetically, I grabbed at the sides of the metal mothership, trying to slow down my descent.

I heard the metal screeching as the claws of my mind held on to it. And soon, I came to a total stop.

But I heard a whooshing sound, and I knew Alternate Kyle was right over my shoulder.

I spun around and immediately blasted three bolts of energy toward him.

He dodged them, like they were nothing more than balloons.

He landed on me then and grabbed my chest. He pulled me in his direction, staring into my eyes. "That's your problem, at this stage of your life. You still aren't strong enough. You still don't believe in yourself. Because you're just puny Kyle Peters, and you never stop needing to be Glacies, or Hielo, or one of your many other identities. You try to be strong enough as Kyle Peters, but you always, always end up going back to an alternate identity. And that will be your downfall. Trust me. I know."

He punched me then, right in the middle of my head.

And when my head rolled back, I saw Earth right beneath me.

I saw more of those humans shooting up through those green lights.

And on the surface of the Earth, I saw explosions and storms and lightning.

I saw a world dying.

I couldn't let that happen.

I felt that tingling sensation starting to split through my body. I pulled my head forward, turned to face Alternate Kyle. I could feel the ice forming on my hands, a wormhole opening up behind him. I knew this was it. I knew he didn't understand, somehow. I knew I was strong enough.

"Give up," he said. But there was less certainty to his voice now. "You'll never win."

My entire body vibrated. I focused on those vibrations, readied to unleash the power I was bottling up within. "I'll never give up," I said. "And you'll never—"

Another crack smacked into my face.

In the click of a finger, the vibrations stopped.

My energy stopped.

And I was weak once again.

I gasped, spitting blood from my lips into the floating atmosphere. I tried to trigger the vibrations again—

Another punch, right across my face.

I went dizzy. I started to spit out more blood in my mouth. I could feel something floating around between my lips, and I realized right away that it was a broken tooth.

"This is what you get when you resist the inevitable," Alternate Kyle said.

He punched me again. Hard.

"This is what you get when you fight the truth."

And then another punch. This one even harder. And before

I knew it, I wasn't in space at all, I was with Cassie and Ellicia and Avi and Damon and Dad and everyone, and we were all relaxed, all happy, all...

"This is what you..."

I didn't hear the rest of what Alternate Kyle had to say.

By that point, I was gone.

[47]

Daniel looked at the destruction on Earth and for the first time in a long time, he actually felt afraid.

It was the middle of the afternoon, but it was impossible to tell that from the thick black clouds above. Lightning struck at a rapid pace, slamming into buildings and hitting the surface of the water. There was a constant sound of screaming in the air, which made the hairs on the back of his neck stand on end.

And worst of all?

Those green beams, which were dragging humanity up through, toward whatever the future held for them.

Daniel watched as people were dragged up through those beams. It looked like they were in some kind of trance. And he found himself thankful that they weren't conscious to witness the destruction of Earth. Which was weird in a way, because it made him realize just how far he'd come.

He used to be so hateful of other people. He used to allow himself to be bullied and trodden on, and then when he realized the abilities he was capable of, he lashed back at humanity, hoping to put them all down and rule over the planet for himself.

But that was different, now. And that difference spawned because he'd seen the kindness other people were capable of. He'd seen the levels of forgiveness they were willing to go to.

And sure. People had given him a rough time when he'd been in school.

But they were just bullies.

Bullies were still around. Only now, he'd made it his duty to fight them, instead of lashing out at people who didn't have those tendencies.

He looked from the rooftop of the Rockefeller. Across the city, explosion after explosion. He wanted to fight, like Kyle had told him to. But the truth was, he couldn't. None of them could. Something happened to their abilities the second they returned to Earth's atmosphere. And now, he couldn't even fly. It was like he'd lost control of himself, piece by awful piece.

"Daniel?"

He turned around and saw Stone walking toward him.

He staggered back when he saw what Stone was holding at first. Or rather, *who* Stone was holding.

He knew Kyle would never forgive him.

Ellicia was still on Earth.

She was in Stone's arms. Stone had been pulling her down, stopping her from disappearing into one of those green beams.

Ellicia had gone completely pale. Veiny marks stretched right across her face. She looked ill. Very ill.

"Is she still..." Daniel asked.

Stone nodded. "Just about. But her heartbeat's low."

Daniel's stomach sank. "She's still here at least."

"Daniel, we need to seriously start thinking about—"

"No," he said.

He saw the disapproving looks from the rest of the ULTRAs behind Stone.

Stone shook his head. He was clearly struggling to hold her down himself. Somehow, he'd managed to hold on to some of his abilities. But as for how long that would last... no-one knew.

"It's unfair. Unfair to keep her down here if it's doing her damage."

"I made a promise."

"It's time you reconsidered that pr—"

"No," he said.

He stepped right up to Stone, then, as explosions echoed behind him. The light from the green beam was burning, intense. "We hold onto her. We keep her here. We don't just let her go. We don't give up."

Stone narrowed his eyes. He looked like he was about to make one of those sarcastic, grumpy remarks.

Instead, he just sighed and nodded. "Better hope Kyle comes through. I don't... I don't think I have much longer left."

Daniel turned around and looked up at the sky, right up at that small black dot where he knew the mothership was.

"Come on, Kyle," he muttered, as he heard Ellicia yelp with pain in her state of unconsciousness. "Come on. Please."

[48]

I felt the grip tightening around my neck and I knew I didn't have long left.

All around me, there was darkness. Total darkness, so black it was suffocating. Just looking at that darkness made me feel a wave of sickness and light-headedness, in the way a young kid feared the dark at night. The same reason they begged their parents to keep a night light on for them. There were always monsters in the dark, in the mind of a kid.

Except right now, there really was a monster in this darkness.

And that monster was me.

The grip tightened even harder around my neck. I kicked back, reflexively more than anything. There was nothing else I could do, not really. I'd tried sparking my powers. I'd tried firing my way free of this mess. All of it was to no avail.

I was trapped. And the life was slipping away from me by the second.

I heard the blasts all around me, accompanied by the screams, and the feeling of sickness deep within grew even more intense. I knew where those blasts and screams were coming from. Earth. I could hear Earth hurting, even this far away, right from the mothership.

A bitter taste of blood and vomit filled my mouth, making me want to cough. I could smell something in the air. I couldn't describe it any other way than a thickness. Like the air was filled with tar, and that thickness was getting even more slimy, making breathing gradually more difficult.

But it was the eyes that scared me more than anything.

There was nothing grandiose about these eyes. There was nothing menacing about them, to the average person. It was their familiarity that got to me more than anything. I'd looked into these eyes before, a number of times. I'd stared into them, and they'd stared back at me.

They were my eyes.

And now they were the eyes that were looking at me as I struggled for my final breaths.

"It's over," Alternate Kyle's deep, gruff voice said. "Don't fight it. This is the only way it happens. This is the way it's always happened. Just... release."

I didn't want to stop fighting, as much as giving up any resistance would be the easy option here. So I gritted my teeth and kept my focus on those eyes, like I had so many times already. "N... never."

The hand around my neck loosened just enough for me to catch some breath. I coughed, then I felt vomit trickling up and out of my mouth, stilling my quest for a good lungful of air.

When I'd spewed up, the grip tightened once again, and I was pinned back hard against a solid wall.

As I was held there, I wondered what I had done to deserve this life. I was Kyle Peters. I wasn't even in my twenties, and yet somehow, I was the strongest ULTRA in existence—at least people thought, and at least people expected. I didn't *ask* to be Glacies. Glacies just became me.

I'd been dealt these cards, and now I was being forced to live with them. Now, I was being forced to accept who I was. But also something else.

I was being forced to accept that I wasn't as strong as I'd hoped—or as the world hoped—all along.

"All these years of resisting instead of living," Alternate Kyle said. "Now, it's time to stop. It's time to hand yourself over. So stop resisting, Kyle. End the pain. For yourself. For your family."

The mention of my family made me feel a warmth deep inside. But it was a warmth tinged with sadness. After all, my family had been torn apart, all because of me. It had been decimated, all because of me.

I felt a tear roll down my cheek when I thought of Ellicia, Dad, Damon, Avi, Cassie, Daniel, Orion, and all my old friends from the Resistance. "I can't stop fighting. For... for their sakes. I can't give up."

Alternate Kyle chuckled, then. As he did, the room lit up, and I saw my surroundings for the first time in God-knows-how-long. I was in some kind of dark cavern. It was massive. It stretched as tall as I could see, and the walls were further away than I could perceive. The sheer size of this place was enough to make the hairs on my arms stand on end, purely because something this big wasn't human. It wasn't manmade. It was alien. Totally alien.

The scariest thing about it, though?

That bright light, shining right in the middle of this cavernous void.

And yet...

"I can't give up," I said. "And I won't give up."

I held my breath and thought of all the pain in my life. As I thought of the pain—and there was a lot of it, not least the pain I'd felt these last few days, some of the purest pain of all—I felt my powers getting stronger once again. I could feel them charging up. I could feel the ice creeping down my spine, stretching down my arms, scaling my fingers, tickling my fingertips.

I went to lift my arms and fire at Alternate Kyle.

His grip around my neck loosened completely. I felt my stomach turn as I dropped down below. Immediately, I triggered my flight powers, needing to regain some sense of composure.

But nothing happened.

I was still falling.

I felt my stomach drop as I crashed toward the ground. I shouted out and lifted my hands in the air, trying to fire some kind of ice to the roof of this cavern.

But the cavern walls and ceilings were just too high.

The ice didn't grip with the walls.

I kept on falling.

As I fell, fear filling my body, scrambling from side to side, for a moment, I felt a sense of calm. It was weird and totally unexpected, but it was there.

Calm, because soon, there'd be nothing left of me.

Calm, because I wouldn't have to fight any longer.

And, ultimately, the position of not having to fight any longer was what I'd been striving toward all this time, right?

The cavern floor grew rapidly closer as I hurtled through the air toward it.

Sadness filled my body. I felt more tears roll down my cheeks, my throat wobbling. "I love you..." I started, intending to say "Mom" or "Dad" or "Ellicia" or anyone after it.

But in the end, there were so many people I loved that I couldn't say a thing.

I looked up. Above, I saw that total pitch black darkness again.

I felt the fear creeping up into my chest.

I held my breath.

Then, I fired one last shot of ice right up toward the ceiling.

I stopped.

Confusion filled my body. I spun left and right, still gasping in the darkness as I hovered there, totally static. *Did I do it? Did the ice stick?*

Then the face appeared in front of me all over again.

They were smiling, now. I could tell they were smiling because they didn't have their mask on, not anymore.

Their smile made my body shake. I tried to look away, but I couldn't. It was like they had me wrapped up in some hypnotic trance.

They grabbed my neck again. I battled for that final breath. I didn't get a lungful.

"You should've given up when I gave you the opportunity," Alternate Kyle said. "You were a fool for fighting. Now, we do things the hard way."

Alternate Kyle stretched out his hand and pressed it against my chest.

Immediately, I felt a searing pain stretch through my body, and I lurched from side to side. "You won't win!" I shouted. "You'll never win!"

Alternate Kyle smiled again, his hand still pressed against my chest. "That's where you're wrong, Kyle Peters. And this is where it ends for you, I'm afraid. It's been nice knowing you. But really, it's time."

The burning sensation in my chest spread right across my body. I tried to spark my powers, but the burning just seemed to melt my ice right away. I tried to teleport, but I couldn't. I was just too weak.

"You won't win," I shouted. "You won't..."

There was nothing else to say. I didn't even have the strength to speak now.

Alternate Kyle pushed his hand further into my chest.

More pain.

More fear.

More weakness.

I saw a light blue glow illuminate in front of me, then. I felt sick right away. I knew what this was.

The end.

My defeat.

My imminent destruction.

"You've already lost," Alternate Kyle said, dragging the blue light from my body like he was taking away my innards. "Goodbye, Kyle Peters. Goodnight. This is where your story ends."

The last of the blue light was dragged from my body.

This is where your story ends...

I was starting to believe it, as my body gave up fighting, and darkness closed in.

BUT THEN SOMETHING HAPPENED.

I opened my eyes.

I wasn't sure what gave me the strength to just open my eyes. It didn't feel like any kind of grand gesture. It just felt like... well, like what I *had* to do.

When I opened my eyes, I saw Alternate Kyle hovering opposite me.

He was holding his fists together. I couldn't breathe, so I figured he was suffocating me.

And yet, somehow, it just didn't matter.

It didn't matter because I wasn't afraid anymore.

Somehow, I wasn't afraid...

I lifted a hand then, my heart pounding.

I put it on my neck and gripped at the invisible, telekinetic force wrapped around it.

I dug my nails in. I dragged it away. And as I did, I saw the confusion on Alternate Kyle's face. As far as he was concerned, this wasn't supposed to happen. This wasn't how it ended.

He tightened his grip.

For a split second, I did feel weaker.

But then I didn't let that fear take hold of me.

Instead, for the first *real* time, I believed.

I was Kyle Peters.

I was strong.

Just as I had that thought, the grip loosened from around my neck.

Theoretically, if we talk physics, I should've dropped down to whatever fate lay below me.

Instead, I stayed hovering on the spot.

Alternate Kyle narrowed his eyes. "What..."

I smiled at him.

Then he lifted his hands, and a load of crafts appeared behind him.

I looked at each and every one of them. For a second, I felt that fear again, right in the pit of my stomach.

But as those crafts surrounded me, as Alternate Kyle hovered opposite me, and as the light beamed behind him, I just exhaled, and reminded myself I didn't have to be afraid.

"That's the difference between you and me," I said. I could feel the tingling sensation filling my body. Only this time, it was stronger than it had ever been.

He narrowed his eyes. Then he pointed right at me. "Get him."

The crafts came flying toward me, firing, slicing with their tentacles.

I didn't even have to jump around and dodge them.

I just lifted a hand and moved it in front of me.

I felt that tingling energy, and I had it under control now. I watched as those crafts disintegrated, one by one, until there was nothing left in this enormous room but me and my future self.

"You aren't my future self," I said.

He tried to fire some ice at me, but I stopped it.

And then when he tried again, I paralyzed him right there in the air.

I floated toward him, my heart racing at three hundred beats per minute. I looked down at my chest, and I saw a light. My power. It was right on the surface now. It was on the verge of exploding.

But I had it. For now, I had it.

"You were right about one thing," I said, as I hovered closer to Alternate Kyle. "I'm not supposed to make it past this point. And that's why you shouldn't be here, right now."

I saw the fear in his eyes. Almost like he was understanding what I was saying, after all this time.

I smiled at him then, and I felt a tear roll down my cheek. "But you were wrong when you said I wasn't strong enough. Because I am strong enough. I don't need Glacies to be strong. I don't need Hielo to be strong. And as much as you think ULTRAs will lead to the downfall of man, you don't get to make that decision. Not now."

The burning energy seared out of my skin. I was completely covered in light now. I knew it was close.

I grabbed Alternate Kyle by his arms.

Then I floated both of us right toward that huge ball of energy, burning so bright that I knew that even if I looked away from it, I'd never be able to see again.

Alternate Kyle tried to shake free. He tried to fight back.

But my powers were too strong.

They were stronger than he was.

I was stronger than he was.

We got right to the edge of the ball of energy, then, and all I could see was light. But I could feel that I was heading in the right direction.

I was sad that I'd never look back and see Earth again.

I was sad that I'd never have a chance to say a proper goodbye to Ellicia, Avi, Dad, and everyone else—all of my friends.

I was sad about a lot of things.

But most of all, I felt strong.

I was Kyle Peters, and I was saving the planet.

"Goodbye," I whispered, as I held my future self up to the ball of energy.

I felt him struggle violently for a few seconds. Then I heard cracks and explosions and saw electricity.

I knew I didn't have long.

Tears streamed down my cheeks. My bottom lip shook. Every instinct in my body told me to back away.

But I knew that I couldn't.

I couldn't, because this was how it was meant to be.

I couldn't allow Alternate—or Future—Kyle to come back.

And that meant this was the moment I made my greatest sacrifice.

I saw Ellicia in my mind. Her dark hair. Her cheeky smile. I saw us holding hands for the first time, going on our first date. I saw the late nights we'd spend just lying next to each other, listening to one another breathe.

I saw Dad, then. The times he'd picked me up when I was low. The amount of belief he'd given myself. And the smile on his face when Cassie was returned to him—the smile on my face, Damon's face, Avi's face, Ellicia's face—as we all came back together.

And then I saw Mom and Damon, holding out a hand, waiting for me.

"I'm ready now," I muttered, as the burning light singed my body. The energy inside me was at bursting point, ready to go off like a nuclear bomb.

Mom smiled.

Damon waved a hand at me, beckoning me to follow.

"I'm ready," I said.

I saw myself in my mind's eye. This time, I wasn't wearing my Glacies gear. I wasn't hiding behind any other identity.

I was just me. Kyle Peters.

And in that instant, I felt so proud.

"I'm ready."

I clenched my teeth together.

Held my breath.

Then I closed my eyes and I let the energy inside me released stronger than ever before.

For a second, I felt burning. I felt sheer, total agony.

And then I felt calm and peace as my body exploded with light.

"I'm ready..." I screamed.

And then, after the explosion of light, there was silence.

[49]

Stone held on to Ellicia, but he could feel himself getting weaker and weaker.

The sky had turned completely black. Not even the lightning was enough to spark up any light anymore. All around him, he watched as the city was torn up, and he knew this building they were standing on could be next.

The only thing he could see?

The humans, traveling up that green light, toward whatever fate and future lay ahead.

He clenched his grip on Ellicia, but in all truth, he was worried for many reasons. He could taste the metallic tang of blood on his lips. His head was aching from all the pressure he'd applied over the last couple of hours. His entire body, which was still covered in stone, was shaking now.

He didn't want to let go, but he knew that he was getting weaker. He was amazed he'd been able to hold onto his powers for this long as it was. All of the others had long ago lost use of their abilities. Perhaps he was even stronger than he thought.

There was another more primary worry for him right now

though, and that was Ellicia herself. She had turned completely purple. Blood was dripping from the corners of her eyes and her lips. Her heart was still beating, and she was breathing. But seeing her like this just wasn't fair.

He'd made a promise to Kyle to hold onto her.

But if he saw her like this... surely he'd let her go, too?

He looked to his left and saw Roadrunner, Daniel, and Cassie both staring at him. They looked at him like they knew what he was thinking. Daniel didn't want Stone to let go for anything. Cassie, she had been more sympathetic.

"I can't keep holding on," Stone said, shaking his head. "I can't keep—"

A bang.

He fell to the left.

Ellicia slipped from his grip.

He jumped up and grabbed her by the ankle before she could disappear into the sky.

It took him a few seconds to realize what'd happened. The building had snapped in two. They were drifting, all of them toward the sky. Except... no. The roof of the building beneath Stone's feet was cracking away. He was being weighed down back toward the earth, just as the rest of his fellow ULTRAs were.

If he didn't let go of Ellicia, he was going to tear her leg off.

He shook his head, then. He looked up at the light, the way the humans were moving so peacefully up in, and he wondered whether that fate for Ellicia would really be so bad after all.

"I can't hold on," he said.

"You keep holding on," Daniel said.

Stone tried to grip harder, but then he realized something was happening.

The stone was receding on his body.

He was being replaced by muscle. Human muscle.

His powers were fading.

He looked at Daniel, at Cassie, and he shook his head. "I'm sorry," he said. "It's over."

"No!" Daniel shouted.

He tried to run at Stone, but then he fell when a chunk of the building cracked away.

Stone was on his own now. He was still holding on to Ellicia. But his grip was loosening. He knew it was time to let go.

"I'm sorry, Ellicia," he muttered. "And... and Kyle. Kid, wherever you are, I'm sorry. But I tried. I tried..."

He closed his eyes.

Then he let go.

He waited for Ellicia to go floating off peacefully into the sky.

But she didn't.

Instead, she fell back down onto Stone and knocked him onto his back.

And then the piece of rubble Stone was floating on fell too.

He felt himself falling through the sky, hurtling back to Earth. In that blink of a moment, he saw the green lights fading too, and the humans tumbling slowly back down. The dark sky broke. Everything cleared.

And something else, too.

Stone was hovering.

He was using his powers, stone covering his body, and he was hovering just above the ground.

He looked at Ellicia, who was in his arms now. Her cheeks were pale, but she wasn't purple anymore, and not being purple was damned something.

He stood together with the rest of the Resistance and looked up at the sky. The sun broke through the clouds. Sure, the city was just rubble. But rubble was better than nothing.

All around, he could see people on their backs. They were

waking up, coughing, looking around with confusion. It would be confusing, probably for a long time. Rebuilding wasn't gonna be easy. There were gonna be hurdles.

But they'd overcome them. Because their resilience was unmatched.

"Is that..." Cassie said.

Stone felt his stomach sink. It was bittersweet, in a way, as they looked up into the sky at that bright white light. It was like a star, only much bigger, and twinkling away. It was right where the darkness of the mothership had been not long ago. It was the brightest, lightest thing he'd ever looked at.

He put a hand on Cassie's back, pulled her in close. "I think it is," he said. "I think... I think your brother did it."

They all came together, then. Roadrunner. Daniel. Cassie. Stone. They held one another. All of them cried. Even Stone cried, dammit.

"Thanks, kid," Stone muttered, as he stood there, Ellicia in his arms. "Thank you."

They would go on to help the rest of the people around them. They'd get people to safety, help rebuild this city, help rebuild the world.

But for now, they stood together, and they felt like Kyle was with them all along.

They saw dust falling from the sky. Light specks of dust. And as it fell, it felt like they were being sprinkled with just a fraction of his powers.

But as they stood there, together, they looked up at that star and they knew exactly what they were looking at.

The ultimate sacrifice.

A legendary act of bravery.

Kyle Peters.

Not Glacies. Not anything else.

Kyle Peters.
ULTRA.
Hero.

[50]

Five years later

Ellicia looked out of the window of her sixteenth story office in London, UK, and wished today was done with already.

It was a pleasant early summer's day. "Pleasant" being a very British way to describe the weather, particularly the summer, which wasn't ever anything to sing about. But today was particularly nice. The sun simmered against the River Thames. Big Ben looked beautiful—albeit nowhere near as big as she'd imagined before she first visited London. The reconstructed London Eye Ferris wheel stood taller and prouder than it ever had before. Really, today was quite the picture.

But Ellicia couldn't wait to get home.

She heard the tapping of keys, and smelled the fumes from the coffee machines. When she glanced away from the window, Karen—one of her better friends at work—smiled at her. "I'm off, Ellicia." She leaned over, hugged her. "You have a safe trip home and I'll see you in a few weeks, yeah?"

Ellicia hugged her back and smiled. "Can't wait to have you and the girls over stateside."

"Yeah, well I can't wait to sample some of those nightclubs you've been telling me all about."

Ellicia rolled her eyes. "Yeah. Me, the big nightclub fan."

"You aren't convincing anyone. See you soon, hun."

They hugged again, then Karen disappeared and Ellicia suddenly felt very alone at Hogan's Law Firm. She'd been working here for two years now. It wasn't anything special. She'd had an internship after finishing college and decided to move over to the UK for a clean break.

A clean break from what?

Well. From everything.

Five years ago, the world was a very different place.

She scanned down through her emails, glazing over right away as she deleted spam email after spam email. Her mind wandered back to that day five years ago. The day when the mothership had shot those green beams down to Earth, and begun to drag every human away from the surface and to... well, no one knew where to, exactly. Perhaps one day, that place would be discovered. But not now. There was a time and a place for everything, as some of her English friends said.

She didn't remember an awful load from the day itself. Mostly just waking up, seeing the destruction, then the struggle in the days that followed. The estimated cost of damage globally was unprecedented, on a completely different scale to everything that had happened before. As country after country struggled with poverty and famine, it would've been very easy for the world to tear itself apart as it waited to repair itself.

But it didn't.

Instead, humanity realized that it was much, much stronger than it had ever realized. Humanity showed patience—a patience that got it through the toughest of times, and saw it rise out of the other end a much more united, solid front.

Of course, the ULTRAs helped with the rebuilding. But they were just there to do just that—help.

Humanity led the forefront of the rebuilding process.

How in Kyle's image that was, after all.

She got up from her desk when she'd finished—a stretch of time that dragged on way longer than she could've imagined—then said her goodbyes to the rest of her colleagues before heading straight for an Uber to London Heathrow. She waited even longer in the airport, and after some struggles where she thought she wasn't going to make her plane on time, she was soon boarding the 17:59 to New York JFK, where she arrived at nine p.m. local time eight hours later.

When she got to the airport, her heart picked up as she looked around, passing by all the unfamiliar faces. She was struck right away by just how television-like the American accent was, and how much less performance-oriented Britain was. Not a criticism either way, just an observation. If anything, her year in Britain had made her more subdued.

She searched for a long time for the person picking her up. It wasn't going to be her parents. They were living over in Michigan now, where she'd fly in two weeks after spending some time back where she considered "home". They were heading to New York a week today. She hadn't told them she was heading back a week early, because they'd have just shown up without invite, then.

She wanted a little time alone here, to reflect.

She wanted time with friends.

That's when she saw him.

"Ellicia!"

He was taller, and a lot slimmer, credit to him. He had a

new turban—jet green—and he was waving at her, that big grin on his face.

Ellicia walked up to him and hugged him, beaming from cheek to cheek. "Avi," she said.

"How you doing, girl?"

"'Girl?' Is that another one of those tags you learned from a book?"

Avi's face shifted. "Well. I guess I..."

Ellicia punched Avi playfully. "I'm just joking. It's good to see you, Avi."

He smiled again, looking much more relaxed now. "You too. Girl."

They reminisced about the last three years of their lives as they made their way to Avi's car. Avi was still single, but insisted that his conquest to find love was "stronger than ever." Avi asked whether Ellicia was single, to which she queried whether he was hitting on her, and everything got a bit awkward for a while then.

And that awkwardness led to something else. The inevitable question.

"Why haven't you been to New York in three years, then?"

Ellicia lowered her head. She didn't know what to say. Not really. After all, what *was* her real reason? Fear? Sadness? Something else?

In the end, she decided just to let the first thing that came into her head out, trusting its honesty. "I guess... I guess coming back here meant accepting that he was gone. Because whenever I'm here... I dunno. I guess I see sights and hear things that just remind me too much."

Avi kept his hands on the wheel as they maneuvered their way through the New York traffic, heading in the direction of Staten Island. He spoke about his job as a game designer, how much he loved it, how much of a blast it was. The lights of

Manhattan lit up the night sky bringing so many memories of young love. How long would it have lasted if things had been different? Would they still be together, to this day?

"I get that," Avi said. "Really. I mean. I lost Damon. I lost Kyle. And I lost... I guess I lost you too. So I feel it."

Ellicia felt guilty then. It was a guilt that led her to reach her hand onto the back of Avi's and hold onto it. "Well, I'm here now, Avi."

He glanced away from the road and smiled at her.

Then he looked back ahead and pointed. "Shit. Here it is. Hold on tight."

Avi took a turn down a road that was barely a road. They drove away from the city lights, heading upstate, into the darkened forests.

"Not planning on murdering me, are you?" Ellicia asked.

"Damn. You're onto me. Might as well get it done with."

After forty-ish minutes of driving, they stopped. Ellicia got out of the car, inhaling the fresh country air. The crickets sang, and the light breeze brushed against the trees. So many memories filled her mind.

Avi walked beside her pointing ahead again. "It's not too far. Just over—"

"Don't worry," Ellicia said. "I remember exactly where it is."

Avi smiled then, like he realized he was being stupid. "Of course. Course you do."

They walked through the trees, enclosed by even more darkness. As they moved, Ellicia found herself thinking of the ULTRAs. Although they'd been a great presence in the days of the cleanup, they had drifted into the background since. They'd become something of a legend. They were still out there; no one doubted that, but their numbers seemed limited. Stone had gone off the radar. Roadrunner was nowhere to be seen. As for Orion, Saint, and Daniel... no-one could say.

But one thing was for sure—history had remembered them fondly. An important lesson to bear in mind, should any ULTRA-related events unfold once again.

For now, the world was peaceful.

That was the important thing.

"I should warn you," Avi said, as he waded over the branches that had fallen to the grass. "It might get you kinda... well, I don't wanna say I cried when I first saw it, but..."

He stopped talking, then. Or maybe he didn't. Maybe he carried on, and Ellicia just didn't hear it.

All she could do was focus ahead.

Focus on what was right in front of her.

Lit up in the darkness, there was a statue. It stood tall, with its back to her right now, arms by its sides, fists tensed, and a hood covering its body.

It was larger than life-size. But there was no denying who this was.

Ellicia felt herself welling up already as she walked around it. She'd heard that the memorial had been erected just two years ago, after so long of crafting. She'd seen images of it online. But she'd never brought herself to face it in the flesh. She'd never found the courage to look it in the eye.

And as she walked around the front of it, she still wasn't sure whether or not she was strong enough or courageous enough to face it, head on, and accept the truth.

Avi took her hand in his. He smiled at her. "Come on," he said. "It'll help. I swear."

Ellicia took a shaky breath.

You can do this. You can do this.

Then, she stepped around the front of the memorial.

When she looked up at it, she couldn't comprehend what she was looking at, initially. It was... so perfect. So *real.*

Kyle's face, in all its glory, imprinted onto that statue,

looking out over the beautiful view from the hills of Manhattan, like he was guarding the world even though he was gone.

On the stone beneath it, an engraving.

Kyle Peters.

RIP.

A Hero Once, A Hero Forever.

But the most beautiful thing of all?

The bright light above his head. The star in the night sky.

Nobody could explain why that star was there. They'd tried to send small crafts up there to look at it closer, but strangely, it vanished when you got near to it, kind of like a rainbow.

But that light was engrained on the outside of the Earth's atmosphere. And it was looking down on the world, right above the statue's head.

The brightest of lights, visible even in the day.

The light from the end of the battle.

The light that came from Kyle when he sacrificed himself to save the planet.

"Well?" Avi said. Ellicia could hear his voice breaking. "Whaddya think?"

She felt her lips wobbling too, and there was no disguising the truth anymore. "Oh, Avi."

She held him, and he held her back. She felt safe in the warm arms of her friend, and she knew he must do too. What they had between each other was special. They'd seen so much. They'd *been* through so much. Even when Kyle was away, fighting, Avi had always been there.

And that bond, that friendship, it would never go away. It would never be replaced.

"I'm sorry I took so long to come home," Ellicia said.

"Hey," Avi said. He squeezed Ellicia a little tighter and lifted her off the ground. "I'm just glad you're here now."

She looked into his eyes and for a moment, she wondered. Could it work? Could something work between them?

And then the moment passed, and they hugged each other again.

Their friendship was strong. It would always bind them. Nothing would get in its way.

They sat on the hillside in the shadow of the statue and the memorial for a while until the lights of the grounds went off. But that light above stayed lit, as did the lights of the city. Ellicia could hear the sounds of the city in the distance, but mostly things were silent. Peaceful.

"Do you ever wonder sometimes if..." Avi started. "If he's still out there, somewhere?"

Ellicia picked at the grass beneath her. She had thought about this, of course. But she hadn't really entertained that it could be possible. So what did she say?

What did she really think?

She took a deep breath; then she looked up at the statue of Kyle's face.

Then, she looked at the blinking star, which shimmered in the sky.

"Even if he's not," she said, "he'll always be with us. He'll always be remembered. For what he did."

The pair of them stayed there a little while longer, until it got colder. Ellicia didn't realize how long, until Avi had a hand on her shoulder, and she realized she'd been drifting off.

"Come on, jet lag," he said. "Let's get you home."

Ellicia laughed. "Yeah. I guess I should've thought about sleeping at some point. I've got to go see Cassie tomorrow. Want to be fresh and ready for that."

They walked down the hill, toward Avi's car.

Before they reached it, Ellicia felt an icy cold breeze on the back of her neck and heard an inaudible whisper. It was strange. Indescribable.

She turned around.

There was no one there.

Just the statue of Kyle.

Above it, the light, twinkling brighter in the sky.

She stared at that light for a while, watching its twinkles, its flashes.

Then she smiled. "Thank you," she said. "Always."

She turned around, and she made her way to Avi's car, ready to continue her trip back to New York, to the States, and ready to continue her life, once and for all.

And for one brief, fleeting moment, the wind blew bitter cold, and the fingertips of Kyle's statue went icy, as the star expanded and twinkled brighter than it ever had before.

WANT MORE FROM MATT BLAKE?

If you want to be notified when Matt Blake's next novel is released, please sign up for the mailing list by going to: http://mattblakeauthor.com/newsletter Your email address will never be shared and you can unsubscribe at any time.

Word-of-mouth and reviews are crucial to any author's success. If you enjoyed this book, please leave a review. Even just a couple of lines sharing your thoughts on the story would be a fantastic help for other readers.

mattblakeauthor.com
mattblake@mattblakeauthor.com

Made in the USA
Coppell, TX
09 November 2021